THE UNAVOWABLE COMMUNITY

THE
UNAVOWABLE
COMMUNITY

Maurice Blanchot

translated by Pierre Joris

BARRYTOWN
STATION HILL

Originally published in French under the title *La Communauté Inavouable*,
copyright © 1983 by Les Editions de Minuit.

Published by Station Hill Press, Inc., Barrytown, New York 12507,
with grateful acknowledgement to the National Endowment for the Arts,
a federal agency in Washington, D.C., and the New York State Council
on the Arts, for partial financial support of this project.

Produced by the Institute for Publishing Arts, Barrytown, New York
12507, a not-for-profit, tax-exempt organization.

Cover design by George Quasha and Susan Quasha.
Text design by Susan Quasha.
Type by Studio 31/Royal Type.

Library of Congress Cataloging-in-Publication Data

Blanchot, Maurice.
    [Communauté inavouable. English]
    The unavowable community / by Maurice Blanchot; translated by
Pierre Joris.
    p.   cm.
    Translation of: La communauté inavouable.

    1. French literature — 20th century — History and criticism.
2. Community in literature.   I. Title.
PQ307.C57B55 1988
840'.9'355 — dc19

CONTENTS

THE UNAVOWABLE COMMUNITY

TRANSLATOR'S PREFACE

Maurice Blanchot's *The Unavowable Community* is a major addition to an *oeuvre* now spanning half a century. Although the theme of community — from the limited community of two (lovers, friends) to some more encompassing social community — has never been absent from his work, the present book is the first explicit discussion of community, bringing together and carrying forward the various strands of his political, social, literary and philosophical thinking. It is, at one and the same time, a re-orchestration of old themes and a new quite personal re-thinking of issues deeply important to him. It is also in some respects the most personally revealing piece of writing we have by this notoriously reclusive author, a spiritual and intellectual disclosure that does not depart from his most distinctive strategies, i.e., Blanchot reveals by not revealing, unconceals even as he conceals.

The first part of his book, "The Negative Community," arose as a response to Jean-Luc Nancy's *La Communauté Désoeuvrée*[1] — a meditation on certain essential themes in the work of Georges Bataille, while the second part is a reading of, commentary on, *La Maladie de la Mort*, a short fiction by Marguerite Duras.[2] The juxtaposition of Bataille and Duras is not as haphazard as it may appear at first glance. Duras was one of the first writers of her generation to seriously read Bataille (in the forties and fifties it was Sartre and Camus who held the attention of most young writers, while Bataille's reputation remained as secret as it had always been). She interviewed Bataille in 1957 for the journal *France Observateur*, and a year later contributed a perspicacious essay to the first (and only) issue of the magazine *La Ciguë*, one of the first magazines to dedicate a whole issue to Bataille's work (other contributors included René Char, Louis-René des Forêts,

Michel Leiris, Jean Fautrier, André Masson, André Malraux and Jean Wahl). In that essay, she calls Bataille's work, "a writing against language," going on to say that "he invents how not to write while writing." Duras' sense of the *récit*, especially the one under consideration here, although written in 1982, owes much to Bataille's writing and thinking, as Blanchot saw immediately (and as she herself would probably acknowledge). Morever, Blanchot's own sense of the *récit*, or more exactly, of the *narrative voice*, as defined in the 1964 essay of that title (included in the *The Gaze of Orpheus*[3]), draws on Duras' writing, as the following quote from that essay, subtitled "*the 'he,' the neuter*," makes clear:

> [The narrative voice] is a voice that has no place in the work but does not hang over it either, far from falling out of some sky under the guarantee of some superior Transcendence: that "he" is not the "encompassing" of Jaspers, but rather a kind of void in the work — the absence-word that Marguerite Duras describes in one of her tales (*récits*): "a hole-word, hollowed out in its center by a hole, by the hole in which all the other words, should have been buried," and it goes on: "One could not have spoken it, but one could have made it resound — immense, endless, an empty gong . . . ." It is the narrative voice, a neuter voice that speaks the work from that place-less place in which the work is silent.

That Blanchot should come back to Duras in the context of a book like *The Unavowable Community* is not surprising: much of Duras' best writing — especially the *récits* — is not only close to Blanchot's sense of literature, but also often poses, at least implicitly, the question of the possibility of community. However her own sense of "community" probably has its deepest roots in her actual experience of the "secret community" of the Resistance during World War II (cf., for example, her 1986 interviews with François

Mitterand in the excellent but short-lived magazine *L'Autre Journal*). "The Community of Lovers," the essay on Duras' text, presents relatively few problems of translation or understanding. While taking up some of the thinking concerning Bataille first presented in the opening essay, it is in the main a straightforward — if that term has any meaning in relation to Blanchot — reading of the Duras text, a meditation on the possibility of a restricted community of two — lovers or friends. The reader should keep in mind the great importance Blanchot attaches to friendship, despite the public image of a solitary and secretive personage which he has encouraged for most of his life. It is not for nothing that he gives the title of a small essay honoring Georges Bataille to his 1971 collection, *L'Amitié*, "Friendship." This title, in turn, echoes the subtitle of Georges Bataille's essay *Le Coupable*.[4]

There can be no doubt that for Blanchot friendship is profoundly linked to the possibility of community. That death, disaster, absence are at the core of this possibility of community — making it always an impossible, absent community — is, in effect, the central thrust of *The Unavowable Community*. Some of these links can be glimpsed in the following extracts from letters of Blanchot to Bataille:

> "Let me add that friendship is also the truth of the disaster"; "The thought that you were ill was extremely distressing to me and was like a threat aimed at something that both you and I would hold in common"; "It seems to me that in these days of distress [*détresse*: also anguish, danger] — in this way, ordinary days — something has been given us in common, to which we also have to respond commonly . . ."; "That something which one may call misfortune (*malheur*), but which one also has to leave nameless, can, in a certain way, be common. Which is mysterious, maybe a delusion, maybe unutterably true."[5]

"The Negative Community," the essay dealing with Nancy's text, presents a number of more or less arduous reading and translation problems. It is probably one of Blanchot's most complex pieces, concatenating as it does philosophy, sociology, literary history, politics, and personal (not to say private) reflections. By no stretch of the imagination could any of Blanchot's writings be described as easy to read, a fact that has led at least one supercilious critic to pun on the title of his first book and refer to him as "Blanchot l'Obscur." But Blanchot is never obscure for the sake of obscurity. Rather, he is true to the nature of difficult, nearly *unspeakable* questions, of literally *unthinkable* concerns such as *absence* and *silence*. The unavoidable difficulty of his text presents special problems to the translator, by no means limited to the choice of the right words in English (though this problem is considerable). In the present text, even more than elsewhere, the processual nature of his writing and thinking makes for writing that is syntactically dense even as it quickly shifts levels of discourse, aiming to carry forward Blanchot's many-layered concerns.[6]

However a more immediate difficulty for the American reader might be the number of shorthand references to French literary, philosophical and political history of the past fifty years. Rather than encumbering an already dense text with editorial notes, it has seemed more advisable to provide some of the necessary context in this preface. Nancy's essay essentially consists in an analysis of a sense of loss of community reflected in Georges Bataille's essays on that subject. Bataille and Blanchot first met in 1941 (i.e., *after* Bataille's "communitarian" involvements described below) and, writes Bataille, there was "immediate admiration and agreement" between the two men. Bataille's thought has clearly exercised an abiding influence on Blanchot over the years — if, in a writer so profoundly original, one can speak of influence at all. Relatively little of Bataille's writing was published during his own lifetime, and after his death in 1962 his work passed through a kind of *purgatorio*, ending in 1970 when Gallimard began publishing his Collected Works. Although he is now recognized as one of the major French thinkers of the century, his work is still only partially translated. Of his large output — the Gallimard edition of his collected works consists so far of nine volumes of roughly 500 pages each, with the final three volumes to be published later this year — no more than four or five books are presently available in English. For reading Blanchot's essay, the most useful Bataille is the collection of essays entitled *Visions of Excess*.[7]

As Blanchot points out, it is during the 1930s that Bataille deals most explicitly with the concept of community, both in his writings and in his life. During that period he founded or was active in at least three groups, each very different in conception and aim, though each in its way an attempt to counter the threat of both fascism and bureaucratic Stalinism. The first of these groups was Contre-Attaque, which strangely enough he cofounded in 1935 with his old enemy André Breton (a truce between the two men that did not last long) and which coincided "with the greatest period of political effervescence in France since the Paris Commune of 1871" (Stoekl), culminating in the Popular Front government, an antifascist alliance of Socialists and Communists led by Léon Blum. In 1934 the fascist paramilitary organizations had taken to the streets in an attempt to overthrow parliamentary democracy. The CGT (the Communist Union) fought back by creating a Vigilance Committee and by calling for a general strike. Contre-Attaque, "the revolutionary intellectuals' combat union," was born from this upheaval a year later when Breton, who had just broken with the French Communist Party, and several of his friends (Eluard, Pastoureau, Peret) joined forces with Boris Souvarine and Georges Bataille. A manifesto, published on October 7, 1935, castigates both capitalism and Léon Blum's Popular Front for its attempt "to avoid the revolution," and states that, given that fascism has used the political weapons created by the workers' movement, the only possible issue is a "completely and totally aggressive revolution." At the point in his essay when he deals with Contre-Attaque, Blanchot uses the term "sur-philosophie" to denote the thought process that led Heidegger to get involved with National Socialism and to differentiate that process from what he calls Bataille's "insurrection of thought." The term plays off Breton's attack on Bataille's Contre-Attaque stance, in which Breton accused Bataille of "surfascism." In 1929 or 1930 Bataille had written an essay called "The 'Old Mole' and the Prefix 'Sur'" which criticized that prefix in the word "Surrealism." The essay was meant for publication in the magazine *Bifur*. The latter, however, folded before the piece could appear, and it was finally first published in *Tel Quel* 34 (Summer 1968). (I do not know if Breton had seen the piece at the time of Contre-Attaque.)

The group started publishing a magazine, *Cahiers de Contre-Attaque*, which never got beyond its first issue. Here is how Stoekl sums up Bataille's dilemma at this point in time:

> It must be recalled when reading Bataille's writings from 1935 to 1940 that there is an assumption that democracy in the West is doomed; the choice is between some form of communism and fascism. In this light, Bataille's espousal of a revolution through sexuality and myth takes on added force: faced with a choice between the clear tyranny of fascism and the tendency of bureaucratic Communists to dessicate life —and with democracy not a viable alternative — the only option was to affirm Revolution, while attempting to situate it in relation to values that all 'official' parties refused to consider seriously. Bataille then had two alternatives: either to work somehow in conjunction with the Communists, as a Marxist, a course of action he advocates in "Popular Front in the Street," or to refuse the mode of struggle of the Stalinist Communist party entirely (thereby refusing to be a Communist), while not refusing the

inevitability of a Marxist "end of history" — the position Bataille takes in the Acéphale period.

But the situation is, I believe, even more complex. There can be little doubt that during the thirties, most intellectuals, Bataille and Blanchot included, were at some time or other attracted to the extreme right. Nancy deals head-on with this question in his book (page 46): " . . . In the thirties, Bataille was prey to two preoccupations . . . a revolutionary agitation wishing to give back to revolt that incandescence the Bolshevik state had stolen, and a fascination with fascism, insofar as the latter seemed to indicate the direction, if not the reality, of an intense community given over to excess." That fascination, says Nancy, was due to the fact that fascism *also* seemed to want to bring an answer — "miserably, ignobly — to the already instituted, the already suffocating reign of society," and was "the grotesque or abject final throes of the obsession with communion, crystallizing the motif of its pretended loss and the nostalgia of its fusional image." In that sense, Nancy claims, fascism was an emanation of Christianity, and the whole of modern Christianity was fascinated by it. Therefore "no politico-moral criticism of that fascination can hit the mark if the one who criticizes is not at the same time capable of deconstructing the system of the communion." In later years Bataille acknowledged that among his friends and even in himself there was a "paradoxical fascist tendency." What Bataille, to some extent, and certainly Blanchot in this essay, are attempting is exactly that work of deconstruction. For understandable, even if objectionable reasons, it has taken a long time for anyone to dare open that proverbial can of worms, and much work remains to be done in this area, though Nancy's book is most certainly a major contribution to this line of inquiry.[8]

This second period of Bataille's involvement in creating communities has two facets: a public and a secret one. The public face of Acéphale was a magazine by that title, of which four issues were published between June 1936 and June 1939. André Masson's drawings of acephalic — headless — man illustrate the issues, setting "the proper cosmological-orgiastic tone" (Stoekl). Among contributors were Georges Ambrosino, Pierre Klossowski, Jean Wahl, and Jules Monnerot, although it was Bataille himself who wrote many of the pieces and nearly everything in the last issue. Acéphale marks both the rupture with direct political involvement as represented by the "Contre-Attaque" group and a return to the political via the most burning question of that period: the question of fascism. As Dominique Lecoq writes in a recent issue of *Le Magazine Littéraire*: "It is via Nietzsche's work that [Bataille] engages the fight against fascism and against nationalism — all nationalisms. That choice is not fortuitous: it represents Bataille's mark on the magazine and his conviction that a reading of the German philosopher was 'decisive . . . .' From that point of view *Acéphale* constitutes the accidental surfacing — linked to historical circumstances — of the secret and permanent dialogue that links Bataille's thought to Nietzsche's."

The other facet was a secret community, reflecting Bataille's fascination with marginal groups such as gnostic and other heterodox Christian sects, and his quest at that moment for communitarian forms that would avoid the two-pronged trap described above. As Blanchot points out, little is known of the actual activities of the Acéphale secret society, and those still around who could talk about it tend not to want to do so. Writes Stoekl: "Its main goals were the rebirth of myth and the touching off in society of an explosion of the primitive communal drives leading to sacrifice. Myth, as Bataille states . . ., is the way open to man after the failure of art, science (and scientific notions of causation), and politics to reach these lower — and more 'essential' — human drives, and after their failure as well to lead to a paradoxically rent but 'true' existence." As far back as 1922, Bataille, after first reading Nietzsche's *Beyond Good and Evil*, had written: "Why even consider writing given that my thought — the whole of my thinking — has been so fully, so admirably expressed." Nietzsche's writings were to haunt Bataille for the rest of his life, and the German philosopher is certainly the central point of reference in the Acéphale period, both in the magazine where Bataille tries to extricate Nietzsche from the role the fascists would have him play and in the secret society which, as Stoekl puts it, can be seen as an attempt to found "a Nietzschean 'faith' or even 'church.'" (See also Stoekl's 'From *Acéphale* to the Will to Chance: Nietzsche in the text of Bataille,' in *Glyph* 6 [Baltimore, Johns Hopkins University Press, 1979]). Bataille's own thinking turns around the concepts of expenditure, risk, loss, sexuality, and death. His old fascination with Aztec human sacrifices resurfaces, and the Acéphale secret society, which took to meeting around trees struck by lightning — as points of intersection between the lower chthonian forces and falling higher forces, there was talk of a human sacrifice as the one way of truly creating a community, though this sacrifice was of course never carried out, Bataille arguing that the sacrificer would have to die at the same instant as his victim.

It is during the Acéphale period that Laure, as she was known then and is referred to even today (for example by Blanchot in his essay), died. Her real name was Colette Peignot, and she had been Bataille's companion since 1934. Her collected writings were to be published by her nephew Jérôme Peignot in the seventies, against the express will of her surviving family, and it is now possible to begin to evaluate the depth and importance of their relationship (see for example Dominique Rabourdin's essay in the Bataille issue of *Le Magazine Littéraire*, June 1987). Her death on November 7, 1938 threw Bataille into profound turmoil, though he did continue his involvement with Acéphale as well as being active in the recently founded Collège de Sociologie, the third and last of Bataille's communitarian ventures.

Bataille had founded the Collège together with Roger Caillois and Michel Leiris in 1937, and the first public meeting took place in November of that year. Stoekl writes: "Its activities centered around biweekly lectures given either by the founding members or by invited speakers, such as Alexandre Kojève, Anatole Lewitsky, Pierre Klossowski, and others. The effort here was to redefine a 'science of the sacred,' replacing a narrow functionalist sociology with one that would recognize the importance of the various forms of 'expenditure' not only for 'primitive' societies, but for modern societies as well. Thus the Collège was meant to study the tendencies of man that the Acéphale group hoped somehow to spark." Among those who came to listen to the lectures were such figures as Claude Lévi-Strauss, Jean-Paul Sartre and Walter Benjamin, with the latter even scheduled to give a series of lectures in 1939-40. The war that broke out in September 1939, however, put an end to the Collège .[9]

To complete our sketch of the background to Blanchot's text, there remains for us to define certain special terms. When Blanchot talks of "May," or "May 68," he refers to the student rebellion of that year, which although a world-wide event, took on a truly revolutionary character in France only when the workers came out on the side of the students and staged the largest general strike since the Popular Front. For a few days there was a real chance for an overthrow of the repressive Gaullist government, as De Gaulle actually fled the country and took refuge with the French troops stationed in Germany, leaving France without an effective govern-ment, i.e., in an "acephalic" state. If the revolution aborted it was, yet again, due mainly to the French Communist Party which controlled the workers' movement and at the decisive moment made a deal with De Gaulle behind the backs of both students and workers.

"Charonne" refers to a moment during the Algerian war, when police attacked demonstrators marching in support of an independ-ent Algeria, and nine people were killed on and around the steps of the entrance to the Charonne subway station.

There are two words I have not translated: *jouissance* and *récit*. There does exist an English word "jouissance," current in the Renaissance and used later by some eighteenth-century poets such as William Dodd, and Webster's Third, terming it obsolete, gives its meaning as *use, enjoyment, jollity*. A detailed discussion of the word in its present use can be found in Leon S. Roudiez's introduction to Julia Kristeva's *Desire in Language* (Columbia University Press, 1980) who suggests that a few centuries ago "both French and English cognates had similar denotations covering the field of law and the activity of sex. While the English term has lost most of its sexual connotations, the French term has kept *all* of its earlier meanings." In France the term as used now by Kristeva, Blanchot and others was brought back into current usage by Jacques Lacan in his 1972-73 seminar. Roudiez writes: "What is significant is the *totality* of enjoyment that is covered by the word 'jouissance,' both in common usage and in Lacan; what distinguishes common usage from Lacan's usage . . . is that in the former the several meanings are kept separate and precipitated, so to speak, by the context, whereas in the latter they are simultaneous — 'jouissance' is sexual, spiritual, physical, conceptual at one and the same time." He goes on to say that in the specific case of Kristeva's use, the word implies "total joy or ecstasy (without any mystical connotation); also through the working of the signifier, this implies the presence of meaning (*jouissance* = *j'ouis dire* = I heard meaning), requiring it by going beyond it."

I have also left the term "*récit*" in French, as none of the English words that might be used to translate it — such as narration, story, tale, telling — carries the full meaning intended by Blanchot and others. In this I am following the advice of Jacques Derrida in *LIVING ON, Border lines*, an important essay on Blanchot's *The Madness of the Day*.[10] In a "Note to translators" incorporated in the *Border Lines* section of the essay, Derrida, having remarked on the anagrammatic "version or reversion" of the French words "l'écrit, le récit (and) la série," writes:

How are you going to translate that, *récit* for example? Not as *nouvelle*, "novella," nor as "short story." Perhaps it will be better to leave the "French" word *récit*. It is already hard enough to understand, in Blanchot's text, in French.

For a further discussion of this term I refer the reader to P. Adams Sitney's afterword to Blanchot's selected essays, *The Gaze of Orpheus*. Drawing mainly on Blanchot's essay, "Song of the Sirens," Sitney suggests that, like the novel, the *récit* is a "movement toward an unknown point. But, unlike it, it does not elaborate itself in diversion, in the textured network of interlocked digressions. That which the *récit* approaches is the *récit* itself . . . . It is, then, in Mallarmé's terms, an allegory of itself." He goes on to quote Blanchot: "The tale (*récit*) is not the narration of an event, but that event itself, the approach to that event, the place where that event is made to happen — an event which is yet to come and through whose power of attraction the tale (*récit*) can hope to come into being too." The notion of the *récit* is clearly linked to Blanchot's sense of "narrative voice," and his impassioned foregrounding of the latter in *After the Fact*[11] pays tribute to the primacy he attributes to these two concepts in relation to the very act of writing:

But, before all distinctions between form and content, between signifier and signified, even before the division between utterance and the uttered, there is the unqualifiable Saying, the glory of a "narrative voice" that speaks clearly, without ever being obscured by the opacity of the enigma or the terrible horror of what it communicates.

The term that has caused the greatest problems is without a doubt *désoeuvrement*, and its derivate, *désoeuvré*, which appears in the title of Nancy's essay, but is very much a Blanchot word. The word has at its core the concept of the "*oeuvre*" (work, body of work, artistic work, etc.) and implies a range of meanings:

idleness, a state of being without work, unoccupied, etc. After various attempts to maintain this semantic range (with the option of keeping Lydia Davis' early rendering of the word as "worklessness"), I decided to use the term "the unworking" — first suggested to me by Christopher Fynsk. It is a key term in Blanchot's thinking and it would be useful here to quote certain relevant passages from both Blanchot and Nancy.

The word appears in its common meaning of "idle, at loose ends, finding oneself with nothing to do," etc. in Blanchot's fiction as far back as the 1952 book *Celui Qui Ne M'Accompagnait Pas;*[12] but even here the author playfully worries the word, making it yield a one-page meditation on its meaning and excavating in the process the core-word *oeuvre:*

> Though I did not feel tired, I was disoriented and prodigiously idle [*désoeuvré*]; this idleness [*désoeuvrement*] was also my task, it kept me busy: maybe it represented a lull [*un temps mort*], a moment of giving up and of blacking out on the part of the watcher, a weakness that forced me to be myself all alone. But the empty churning I was caught in had to have another meaning, evoking hunger, evoking the need to wander, to go further, while asking "Why did I come in here? Am I looking for something?," though maybe I was not looking for anything and maybe further on was yet again the same as right here. That much I knew. To know was part of that solitude, created that solitude, was at work [*à l'oeuvre*] in that idleness [*désoeuvrement*], closing off the exits. Out of idleness I asked him . . . .

The full philosophical and literary complexity of the term is worked out later, most fully in the 1969 essay, "The Absence of the Book" (cf. *The Gaze of Orpheus,* pp. 145–160) where Blanchot writes:

> To write is to produce absence of the work (worklessness) [*désoeuvrement*]. Or: writing is the absence of the work as

it *produces itself* through the work and throughout the work.
Writing as worklessness (in the active sense of the word)
is the insane game, the indeterminacy that lies between
reason and unreason.

What happens to the book during this "game," in which
worklessness is set loose during the operation of writing?
The book: the passage of an infinite movement, a movement that goes from writing as an operation to writing as
worklessness; a passage that immediately impedes. Writing
passes through the book, but the book is not that to which
it is destined (its destiny). Writing passes through the book,
completing itself there even as it disappears in the book;
and yet, we do not write for the book. The book: a ruse
by which writing goes towards *the absence of the book.*

It is exactly that little parenthesis, "(in the active sense of the
word)," that is problematic in the translation of the term *désoeuvrement* with the passive "worklessness." (There may be a radical
cultural difference at work here: the puritan impulses of Anglo-
American culture blocking the very possibility of a positive, active
connotation to be attached to the notion of an absence of work?)
All of Nancy's essay builds up to a point, two-thirds of the way
through, where the word "*désoeuvrée*," announced in the title in
relation to community, finally gets stated. It comes after a critique
of the Cartesian immanentist subject, seen by Nancy as "the
inverted figure of the experience of community":

> That is why the community cannot come within the
> province of the work [*l'oeuvre*]. One does not produce it,
> one experiences it as the experience of finitude (or: its
> experience makes us). The community as work, or the
> community through works, would presuppose that the
> common being, as such, is objectifiable and producible (in
> places, persons, edifices, discourses, institutions, symbols:
> in short, in subjects). The products of operations of that

type, no matter how grandiose they want, and sometimes manage, to be, never have more communitarian existence than the plaster torsos of Marianne.

    The community takes place of necessity in what Blanchot has called the unworking [*désoeuvrement*]. Before or beyond the work, it is that which withdraws from the work, that which no longer has to do with production, nor with completion, but which encounters interruption, fragmentation, suspension. The community is made of the interruption of the singularities, or of the suspension singular beings *are*. It is not their work, and it does not have them as it works, not anymore than communication is a work, nor even an operation by singular beings: for it is simply their being — their being in suspension at its limit. Communication is the unworking of the social, economic, technical, institutional work. [13]

After its long incubation in Blanchot's fictions and essays, after Nancy's book and Blanchot's response to it, *le désoeuvrement*, "the unworking" is clearly emerging as one of the most centrally active concepts of contemporary thought not only in relation to the work of writing, but also — as Nancy's last sentence makes clear — in relation to a wide array of other concerns. The necessary tentativeness in the translation of the term is, in a way, proof of the concept's very vitality, that is to say, its active complexity.

    There remains for me to thank all those who have so generously given their time to read and carefully work through this translation: George Quasha, Charles Stein and Christopher Fynsk. Without the careful attention they brought to the manuscript, this translation would be much more imperfect than it is. Of course it is I who am responsible for any remaining errors.

Pierre Joris
Paris/Binghamton
1987/1988

NOTES TO THE PREFACE

[1] Nancy's essay first appeared in issue #4 of the magazine *Aléa*, and was later gathered in book form with two additional and related essays and published in Paris by Christian Bourgois, Editeur, in 1986. An English translation of that book is presently underway and should come out in 1988 or -89 from the University of Minnesota Press. As of this writing, that translation is, however, only in its early stages, and a coordination between the translators was thus not possible.

[2] Translated as *The Malady of Death* by Barbara Bray (Grove Press: New York, 1985). All Duras quotes are from that edition.

[3] Maurice Blanchot, *The Gaze of Orpheus and Other Literary Essays*, Preface by Geoffrey Hartman, translated by Lydia Davis, edited with an Afterword by P. Adams Sitney (Station Hill Press: Barrytown, 1981).

[4] Georges Bataille, *Oeuvres Complètes*, vol. V. (Gallimard: Paris, 1973).

[5] Michel Surya, *Georges Bataille, La Mort à l'Oeuvre* (Librairie Séguier: Paris, 1987). See especially the chapter entitled "La Communauté des Amis" (pp.314-320), from which these quotations are taken. The translation is mine.

[6] There is no easy or "natural" way of translating Blanchot: he seems to inhabit the edges of an invented language, and much as one could claim that every language is always already a second language, his own original is already a translation, or even the translation of a translation. As someone supposedly equally at home in both languages, my work as a translator in relation to this book could best be described as a dialogue between "my own" languages. I use quotation marks advisedly, for the actual act of writing or translating teaches that this someone "equally at home" translates as someone equidistant from both languages, i.e., at a loss in any one language, in exile from that single and fictional "mother-tongue," the "natural" language. No one who writes, and *a fortiori*

no one who translates, is ever "at home" in a language, for all languages are, finally, foreign languages.

[7] Edited, with an introduction, by Allan Stoekl (University of Minnesota Press: Minneapolis, 1986).

[8] On Blanchot's articles in the right-wing press during the late thirties, see also "Blanchot at *Combat*: Of Literature and Terror" in Jeffrey Mehlman's *Legacies of Anti-Semitism in France* (University of Minnesota Press: Minneapolis, 1983).

[9] For more details on the Collège and transcripts of lectures given by Bataille and others, see Denis Hollier's *Le Collège de Sociologie* (Gallimard: Paris, 1979).

[10] This essay was first published in an English translation by James Hulbert in *Deconstruction and Criticism* (Seabury Press, 1979) and has now been included in *Parages*, Derrida's volume of essays on Blanchot (Galilée: 1986); a bilingual version of the essay can be found in *Glyph 7* (Johns Hopkins: Baltimore, 1980).

[11] In *Vicious Circles: Two Fictions and "After the Fact,"* translated by Paul Auster (Station Hill Press: Barrytown, 1985).

[12] (Gallimard; Paris, 1953); to be published shortly by Station Hill Press in a translation by Lydia Davis under the title *The One Who Was Standing Apart From Me*. The occurrence of *désoeuvrement* I am referring to can be found on page 70 of the French edition. Translating *désoeuvrement* with the literary/philosophical term "the unworking" may not work as well in a narrative context. The translation here is mine.

[13] Again, in French the word *désoeuvrement* as used in the last sentence implies an active sense the English "worklessness" does not convey. Another Blanchot translator, Ann Smock, uses the word "uneventfulness" to translate *désoeuvrement*. In a footnote to her translation of *L'Ecriture du Désastre* (University of Nebraska Press: Lincoln, 1986), she writes:

> "The uneventfulness of the neutral wherein the lines not traced retreat" is my elaboration upon Blanchot's expression "*le désoeuvre-*

ment du neutre." *Le désoeuvrement* is a word Blanchot has long used in close association with *l'oeuvre* (the work of art, of literature). It means the work as the work's lack — the work as unmindful of being or not being, as neither present nor absent: neutral. It also means idleness, inertia. My word "uneventfulness" tries to express this idea of inaction, of nothing's happening, and my additional phrase "the lines not traced retreat," recalling an earlier expression in this book, "the retreat of what never has been treated," seeks to retain the relation which this fragment is evoking and which is, so to speak, spelled out in the word *désoeuvrement*: the relation between the work and its denial. Between writing and passivity, between being and not being a writer, being and not being the subject of the verb "to write."

Although I would agree in the main with her understanding of the concept of *désoeuvrement*, I cannot comprehend why she thought it necessary to add the phrase "the lines not traced retreat," which appears to be a translator's interference with the original text. I can only surmise that she felt uneasy with her translation of *désoeuvrement* as "uneventfulness," and therefore wanted to "explain" the term further. Clearly, "uneventfulness" does carry some of the meaning of the French word, though she loses the notion of "*l'oeuvre*," the work.

I

THE NEGATIVE
COMMUNITY

The community of those who do not have a community.
— Georges Bataille

In the wake of an important text by Jean-Luc Nancy, I would again take up a reflection, never in fact interrupted although surfacing only at long intervals, concerning the communist exigency, the relations between that exigency and the possibility or impossibility of a community at a time when even the ability to understand community seems to have been lost (but isn't community outside intelligibility?), and, finally, concerning the flaw in language such words as *communism* or *community* seem to contain, if we sense that they carry something completely other than what could be *common* to those who would belong to a whole, a group, a council, a collective, even where they deny belonging to it, whatever the form of that denial.[1]

COMMUNISM, COMMUNITY

Communism, community: such terms are indeed terms insofar as history, the grandiose miscalculations of history, reveals them to us against a background of disaster that goes much further than mere ruin. Dishonored or betrayed concepts do not exist, but concepts that are not "appropriate" without their proper-improper *abandonment* (which is not simple negation) — these do not permit us to calmly refuse or refute them. No matter what we want, we are linked to them precisely because of their defection. As I write this, I am reading the following lines by Edgar Morin which many of us could make our own: "Communism is the major question and the principal experience of my life. I have never stopped recognizing myself in the aspirations it expresses and I still believe in the possibility of another society and another humanity."[2]

This simple statement may sound naive, but, in its straightforwardness, it expresses exactly what we cannot escape: Why? What about this possibility which, one way or another, is always caught in its own impossibility?

Communism, by saying that equality is its foundation and that there can be no community until the needs of all men are *equally* fulfilled (this in itself but a minimal requirement), presupposes not a perfect society but the principle of a transparent humanity essentially produced by itself alone, an "immanent" humanity (says Jean-Luc Nancy). This immanence of man to man also points to man as the absolutely immanent being because he is or has to become such that he might entirely be a work, his work, and, in the end, the work of *everything*. As Herder says, there is nothing that must not be fashioned by him, from humanity to nature (and all the way to God). Nothing is left out, in the final analysis. Here lies the seemingly healthy origin of the sickest totalitarianism.

Now, this exigency of an absolute immanence implies the dissolution of everything that would prevent man (given that he is his own equality and determination) from positing himself as pure individual reality, a reality all the more closed as it is open to all. The individual affirms himself with his inalienable rights, his refusal to have any other origin than himself, his indifference towards any theoretical dependency in relation to another who

2

would not be an individual as he is, that is to say, in relation to himself perpetually repeated, whether in the past or in the future — thus both mortal and immortal: mortal in his inability to perpetuate himself without alienating himself; immortal because his individuality is the immanence of life which has no limit in itself. (Thus Stirner and Sade, when reduced to certain of their principles, are irrefutable.)

THE EXIGENCY
OF COMMUNITY:
GEORGES BATAILLE

This reciprocity between communism and individualism, denounced by the most austere tenants of counter-revolutionary thought (de Maistre, etc.) as well as by Marx, leads us to question the very notion of reciprocity. However, if the relation of man with man ceases to be that of the Same with the Same, but rather introduces the Other as irreducible and — given the equality between them — always in a situation of dissymmetry in relation to the one looking at that Other, then a completely different relationship imposes itself and imposes another form of society which one would hardly dare call a "community." Or else one accepts the idea of naming it thus, while asking oneself what is at stake in the concept of a community and whether the community, no matter if it has existed or not, does not in the end always posit the *absence* of community. And this is precisely what happened to Georges Bataille who, after having tried for more than a decade, in thought and in practice, to fulfill the exigency of community, did not find himself alone (alone, to be sure though in a shared solitude), but exposed to a community of absence always ready to transmute itself into the absence of community. "Perfect dissoluteness [*dérèglement*] (abandonment to the absence of boundaries) is the rule of an *absence of community*." Or again: "Nobody is entitled

3

not to belong to my *absence of community.*" (Citations from the journal *Contre Toute Attente*). Let us at least keep in mind the paradox introduced here by the possessive adjective "my": how could the absence of community remain mine, unless it be "mine," as *my* death would insist on being a death which can only ruin any belonging to anybody as well as the possibility of an appropriation that is always mine?

I will not take up J.L. Nancy's study at the point where he shows Bataille as the one "who has without a doubt gone furthest in the crucial experience of the community's modern destiny." Any repetition here would oversimplify and thus weaken a thought process which textual citations might modify or even reverse. One must however not lose sight of the fact that one cannot be true to such a thought if one does not take into account Bataille's own infidelity, the necessary mutation which forced him to be unceasingly an other while remaining himself and to develop other exigencies which resisted becoming united either because they responded to the changes of history or to experiences, which, not wanting to repeat themselves, had become exhausted. It is clear that (approximately) between 1930 and 1940, the word "community" imposed itself on his research more than during the following periods, even if the publication of *La Part Maudite* and, later, of *L'Erotisme* (which gives precedence to a certain form of communication) prolongs nearly analogous themes which however cannot be subordinated to what came before (there would be others as well: the unfinished text of *La Souveraineté*, the unfinished text on the *Théorie de la Religion*). One can say that the political exigency was never absent from his thought, though it took on different shapes depending on the interior or exterior urgency. The opening lines of *Le Coupable* speak to this clearly. To write under the pressure of war is not to write about the war but to write inside its horizon and as if it were the companion with whom one shares one's bed (assuming that it leaves us room, a margin of freedom).

4

WHY
"COMMUNITY"?

Why this call from or for "community"? Let me enumerate haphazardly the elements of what was our history. The groups (of which the surrealist group is the loved or hated prototype); the manifold assemblings around ideas that do not yet exist and around domineering persons that exist all too much; above all, the memory of the Soviets, the premonition of what is already fascism but the meaning of which, as well as its becoming, eludes the concepts then in use, forcing thought to reduce it to what is common and miserable in it, or, on the contrary, pointing out what is important and surprising in it, which, not having been well thought out, risks being poorly combatted — and finally (though this could have come at the beginning) the research in sociology which so fascinated Bataille, giving him from the start a certain knowledge as well as a (quickly repressed) nostalgia for modes of being in community, the impossibility of whose implementation in the very temptation they offer us may not be neglected.

THE PRINCIPLE OF
INCOMPLETENESS

I repeat, for Bataille, the question: Why "community"? The answer he gives is rather clear: "There exists a principle of insufficiency at the root of each being . . ." (the principle of incompleteness). Let us take note that what commands and organizes the possibility of a being is a *principle*. It follows that this lack on principle does not go hand in hand with a necessity for completion. A being, insufficient as it is, does not attempt to associate itself with another being to make up a substance of integrity. The awareness of the insufficiency arises from the fact that it puts itself in question, which question needs the other or another to be enacted. Left on its own, a being closes itself, falls asleep and calms down. A being is either alone or knows itself to be alone only when it is not. "Every being's substance is

5

contested without respite by every other being. Even the look that expresses love and admiration attaches itself to me like a doubt touching upon reality." "What I am thinking I have not thought all alone." What we have here is an interweaving of dissimilar motifs which would warrant an analysis, but whose strength resides in the pell-mell of associated differences. It is as if thoughts that can only be thought together crowded around a turnstile, their very multiplicity making any passage impossible. A being does not want to be recognized, it wants to be contested: in order to exist it goes towards the other, which contests and at times negates it, so as to start being only in that privation that makes it conscious (here lies the origin of its consciousness) of the impossibility of being itself, of subsisting as its *ipse* or, if you will, as itself as a separate individual: this way it will perhaps ex-ist, experiencing itself as an always prior exteriority, or as an existence shattered through and through, composing itself only as it decomposes itself constantly, violently and in silence.

The existence of every being thus summons the other or a plurality of others. (This summoning resembles a chain reaction which needs a certain number of elements to be triggered, though it would risk losing itself in the infinite if that number were not determined, just as the universe composes itself only by unlimiting itself in an infinity of universes.) It therefore summons a community: a finite community, for it in turn has its principle in the *finitude* of the beings which form it and which would not tolerate that it (the community) forget to carry the *finitude* constituting those beings to a higher degree of tension.

We are grappling here with difficulties not easily mastered. The community, be it numerous or not (but theoretically and historically there are only communities of small numbers — the community of monks, the Hassidic community [and the kibbutzim], the community of scholars, the community with a view of forming "a community," or the community of lovers), seems to propose itself

6

as a tendency towards a *communion*, even a fusion, that is to say an effervescence assembling the elements only to give rise to a unity (a supra-individuality) that would expose itself to the same objections arising from the simple consideration of the single individual, locked in his immanence.

COMMUNION? That the community may lay itself open to its own communion (which is of course symbolized by all eucharistic communions) is shown by a variety of examples: the group under fascination, as attested by the sinister collective suicide in Guyana; the group in fusion, as named and analyzed by Sartre in his *Critique of Dialectical Reason* (much could be said about this oversimplified opposition of two types of *sociality:* the series — the individual as number; and the fusion — an awareness of freedoms existing only through losing or exalting itself inside a totality in movement); the military or fascist group where each member of the group relinquishes his freedom or even his consciousness to a Head incarnating it without running the risk of being decapitated because it is, by definition, beyond reach.

It is striking that Georges Bataille, whose name for so many of his readers signifies the mystique of ecstasy or the non-religious quest for an ecstatic experience, *excludes* (leaving aside a few ambiguous sentences)[3] "fusional fulfillment in some collective hypostasis" (Jean-Luc Nancy). It is something he is deeply averse to. One must never forget that what counts for him is less the state of ravishment where one forgets everything (oneself included) than the demanding process that realizes itself by bringing into play and carrying outside itself an existence that is insufficient and that cannot renounce that insufficiency, a movement that ruins immanence as well as the usual forms of transcendence. (Concerning this subject I refer the reader to the texts published in *L'Entretien Infini.*)

Therefore (too hasty a "therefore," I admit), the community should not entrance itself, nor should it dissolve its constituent members into a heightened unity which would suppress itself at the same time that it would annul itself as community. It does not follow, however, that the community is the simple putting in common, inside the limits it would propose for itself, of a shared will to be several, albeit to do nothing, that is to say, to do nothing else than maintain the sharing of "something" which, precisely, seems always already to have eluded the possibility of being considered as part of a sharing: speech, silence.

When Georges Bataille evokes a principle of insufficiency, we believe we understand without difficulty what he is saying. It is however not as easy as all that to understand. An insufficiency in regard to what? An insufficiency to subsist? That, clearly, is not the point. Egoistic or generous mutual aid — as can also be seen at work in animal societies — is not even *sufficient* to found the thought of simple gregarious coexistence. The life of the herd may be hierarchical, but that submission of one to another remains a uniformity that never individualizes. Insufficiency cannot be derived from a model of sufficiency. It is not looking for what may put an end to it, but for the excess of a lack that grows ever deeper even as it fills itself up. No doubt insufficiency wants to be contested, but that contention, even if it arose from me alone, is always exposure to some other (or to the other) who is alone able — because of his very *position* — to bring me into play. If human existence is an existence that puts itself radically and constantly into question, it cannot of itself alone have that possibility which always goes beyond it, for then the question would always be lacking a question (self-criticism being clearly only the refusal of criticism by the other, a way to be self-sufficient while reserving for oneself the right to insufficiency, a self-abasement that is a self-heightening).[4]

8

SOMEONE ELSE'S
DEATH

What, then, calls me into question most radically? Not my relation to myself as finite or as the consciousness of being before death or for death, but my presence for another who absents himself by dying. To remain present in the proximity of another who by dying removes himself definitively, to take upon myself another's death as the only death that concerns me, this is what puts me beside myself, this is the only separation that can open me, in its very impossibility, to the Openness of a community. Georges Bataille: "A man alive, who sees a fellow-man die, can survive only *beside himself.*" The mute conversation which, holding the hand of "another who dies," "I" keep up with him, I don't keep up simply to help him die, but to *share* the solitude of the event which seems to be the possibility that is most his own and his unshareable possession in that it dispossesses him absolutely. "Yes, it's true (by what truth?), you're dying. Except that dying, you not only remove yourself, you are also still present, for here you grant me that dying like a granting that surpasses all suffering, and here I tremble softly in what tears, losing speech even as you do, dying with you without you, letting myself die in your place, receiving that gift beyond you and me." To which there is this answer: "In the illusion that makes you live while I am dying." To which there is this answer: "In the illusion which makes you die while you die." (*Le Pas Au-delà*)

THE DYING
PERSON'S
FELLOW CREATURE

That is what founds community. There could not be a community without the sharing of that first and last event which in everyone ceases to be able to be just that (birth, death). What does the community pretend to in its stubbornness to only keep of "you and me" such relations of asymmetry that suspend the *tutoyement* [the

9

that is introduced with it displace authority, unity, interiority by
confronting them with the exigency of the outside which is its
non-directive region? What does the community say if it permits
itself to speak from its boundaries by repeating the discourse on
dying: "One does not die alone, and, if it is humanly so important
to be the dying person's fellow creature, it is, even if in a ridiculous
way, to share the roles and to hold back, to keep from slipping
away, by the gentlest of interdictions, the one who, dying, comes
up against the impossibility of dying in the present. Don't die
now; let there be no now in which to die. 'Don't,' the ultimate
word, the interdiction that becomes complaint, the stammering
negative: don't — you will die"? (*Le Pas Au-delà*)

All this does not mean that the community ensures a kind of
non-mortality. As if it could be said: I do not die because the
community of which I am a part (or the fatherland, or the universe,
or humanity, or the family) goes on. Rather it is almost the exact
contrary. Jean-Luc Nancy: "The community does not create ties
of a higher, immortal or transmortal life, between subjects . . . .
It is constitutionally . . . linked to the death of those one calls,
maybe mistakenly, its members." In effect, "member" refers back to
a self-sufficient unity (the individual) that would associate with
others by contract, or because of inescapable needs, or because of
the recognition of a blood or race relation, or even tribal ties.

COMMUNITY AND
THE UNWORKING

Enjoined [*ordonnée*] to death, the community is not "enjoined to it as to its
work." It does not "*effect* the transfigura-
tion of its dead in any kind of substance
or subject — fatherland, native soil, nation . . . absolute phalan-
stery or mystical body . . . ." I skip a few (quite important)
sentences and come to this affirmation which, for me, is the most
decisive one: "If the community is revealed by the death of the

other person, it is because death is itself the true community of mortal beings: their impossible communion. The community therefore occupies the following singular space: it takes upon itself the impossibility of its own immanence, the impossibility of a communitarian being as subject. In a way the community takes upon itself and inscribes in itself the impossibility of the community . . . . A community is the presentation to its members of their mortal truth (one may say as well that there can be no community of immortal beings . . .). It is the presentation of finitude and of excess without possibility of return that founds the finite-being . . . ."

Two essential traits emerge at this stage of the reflection: 1) the community is not the restricted form of a society, no more than it tends toward a communitarian fusion; 2) it differs from a social cell in that it does not allow itself to create a work and has no production value as aim. What purpose does it serve? None, unless it would be to make present the service to others unto/in death, so that the other does not get lost all alone, but is filled in for [suppléé] just as he brings to someone else that supplementing [suppléance] accorded to himself. Mortal substitution is what replaces communion. Georges Bataille writes: ". . . It is necessary for communal life to maintain itself at the *height of death*. The fate of a large number of private lives is smallness. But a community can last only at the level of the intensity of death; it falls apart as soon as it fails the particular greatness of danger." And one may wish to leave aside certain of these terms, given their connotations (height, greatness), because the community that is not a community of the gods also is neither a community of heroes nor of sovereigns (as in Sade, where the quest for excessive *jouissance* does not have death as a limit, as death given or taken perfects the *jouissance*, just as it comes to completion in sovereignty by closing the Subject in upon himself [where he exalts himself sovereignly]).

11

COMMUNITY
AND WRITING

The community is not the place of Sovereignty. It is what exposes by exposing itself. It includes the exteriority of being that excludes it — an exteriority that thought does not master, even by giving it various names: death, the relation to the other, or speech when the latter is not folded up in ways of speaking and hence does not permit any relation (of identity or alterity) with itself. Inasmuch as the community on behalf of everyone rules (for me and for itself) over a beside-oneself (its absence) that is its fate, it gives rise to an unshared though necessarily multiple speech in a way that does not let it develop itself in words: always already lost, it has no use, creates no work and does not glorify itself in that loss. Thus the gift of speech, a gift of "pure" loss that cannot make sure of ever being received by the other, even though the other is the only one to make possible, if not speech, then at least the supplication to speak which carries with it the risk of being rejected or lost or not received.

Hence the foreboding that the community, in its very failure, is linked to a certain kind of writing, a writing that has nothing else to search for than the last words: "Come, come, you for whom the injunction, the prayer, the expectation is not appropriate."[5] [In the original: "Viens, viens, venez, vous ou toi auquel ne saurait convenir l'injonction, la prière, l'attente."]

If it were permitted — it is not; what I want to say is I lack the means — to follow the windings of Georges Bataille's thought in this evocation of the community, we would discern the following stages: 1) the search for a community, should it exist as a group (in which case its acceptance is bound to an equivalent refusal or rejection): the Surrealist group, nearly all of whose individualities "displease," remains a remarkable attempt in its insufficiency: to belong to it means nearly immediately to form a counter-group, to renounce it violently. 2) "Contre-Attaque" is another group worth studying in detail for what made its urgency of such a nature that it could subsist only through struggle rather than through its non-active existence. It exists, in a way, only in the streets (a prefiguration of what happened in May '68), that is, outside. It affirms itself through tracts that blow right away, leaving no trace. It permits political "programs" to publicize themselves, though what founds it is rather an insurrection of thought, the tacit and implicit answer to the Sur-philosophy that leads Heidegger (momentarily) to not refuse himself to National Socialism and to see in it the confirmation of the hope that Germany will know how to succeed Greece in its predominant philosophical destiny. 3)"Acéphale." It is, I believe, the only group that counted for Georges Bataille and which he kept in mind, over the years, as an extreme possibility. "The College of Sociology," as imperfect as it was, was in no way its exoteric manifestation: the College called for a fragile knowledge, engaging its members, as well as its audience, only in a work of reflection on, and knowledge of, themes partially neglected by the official institutions — themes that were not incompatible with them particularly since the masters of those institutions had been, under various guises, its initiators.

THE ACÉPHALE COMMUNITY

"Acéphale" is still bound to its mystery. Those who participated in it are not certain they had a part in it. They have not spoken, or else the inheritors of their words are tied to a still firmly maintained reserve. The texts published under that title do not reveal its scope, except for a few sentences which much later still stun those who wrote them. Each member of the community is not only the whole community, but the violent, disparate, exploded, powerless incarnation of the totality of beings who, tending to exist integrally, have as corollary the nothingness they have already, and in advance, fallen into. Each member makes a group only through the absoluteness of the separation that needs to affirm itself in order to break off so as to become relation, a paradoxical, even senseless relation, if it is an absolute relation with other absolutes that exclude all relation. Finally, the "secret" — which signifies this separation — is not to be looked for directly in the forest where the sacrifice of a consenting victim should have occurred, a victim ready to receive death from the one who could *give* it to him only by dying. It is too easy to evoke *The Possessed* and the dramatic vicissitudes during which, in order to cement the group of conspirators, the responsibility for a murder committed by one person was destined to enchain one to another all of those who kept their egos in the pursuit of a common revolutionary aim that indeed should have merged them all into one. What we are left with is the mere parody of a sacrifice set up not to destroy a certain oppressive order but to carry destruction into another order of oppression.

The Acéphale community, insofar as each member of the group was no longer only responsible for the group but for the total existence of humanity, could not accomplish itself in only two of its members, given that all had in it an equal and total share and felt obliged, as at Massada, to throw themselves into the nothingness that was no less incarnated by the community. Was it absurd? Yes, but not only absurd, for it meant breaking with the law of the group, the law that had constituted it by exposing it to that which transcended it without that transcendence being other than the group's, i.e., to the outside which was the intimacy of the group's singularity. In other words, the community, by organizing and by giving itself as project the execution of a sacrificial death, would have renounced its renunciation of creating a *work*, be it a work of death, or even the simulation of death. The impossibility of death in its most naked possibility (the knife meant to cut the victim's throat and which, with the same movement, would cut off the head of the "executioner"), suspended until the end of time the illicit action in which the exaltation of the most passive passivity would have been affirmed.

14

SACRIFICE AND
ABANDONMENT

Sacrifice: an obsessive notion for Georges Bataille, but whose meaning would be deceptive if it did not glide continuously from the historical and religious interpretation to the infinite exigency it exposes itself to in what opens it to the others and separates it violently from itself. Sacrifice traverses Madame Edwarda, but does not express itself there. In *Théorie de la Religion,* it is stated: "to sacrifice is not to kill, but to abandon and to give." To link oneself with Acéphale is to abandon and to give oneself: *to give oneself wholly to limitless abandonment.*[6] That is the sacrifice that founds the community by undoing it, by handing it over to time the dispenser, time that does not allow the community nor those who give themselves to it, any form of presence, thereby sending them back to a solitude which, far from protecting them, disperses them or dissipates itself without their finding themselves again or together. The gift or the abandonment is such that, ultimately, there is nothing to give or to give up and that time itself is only one of the ways in which this nothing to give offers and withdraws itself like the whim of the absolute which goes out of itself by giving rise to something other than itself, in the shape of an absence. An absence which, in a limited way, applies to the community whose only clearly ungraspable secret it would be. The absence of community is not the failure of community: absence belongs to community as its extreme moment or as the ordeal that exposes it to its necessary disappearance. Acéphale was the shared experience of that which could not be shared, nor kept as one's own, nor kept back for an ulterior abandonment. The monks divest themselves of what they have, and indeed of themselves, to impart it to the community, which in turn makes them again the owners of everything, with God as guarantor; the same applies to the kibbutz as well as to actual or utopic forms of communism. The Acéphale community could not exist as such, but only as imminence and withdrawal: imminence of a death closer than any proximity; prior withdrawal of that which did not permit one to withdraw from it. Privation of the Head thus did exclude not only the primacy of what the head symbolized, the leader, reasonable reason, reckoning, measure and power, including the power of the symbolic, but exclusion itself understood as a deliberate and sovereign act which would have restored the primacy under the form of its downfall. The beheading, which should have made possible the "endless (lawless) unfettering of the passions," could be accomplished only through passions already unfettered, the passions affirming themselves in the unavowable community that its own dissolution sanctioned.[7]

THE INNER
EXPERIENCE

Acéphale, before coming into being and in the impossibility of *ever* being, thus belonged to a disaster that not only exceeded it and exceeded the universe it was meant to represent, but transcended anything one could name transcendence. It may certainly seem puerile to call upon the "unfettered passions," as if they were, in advance, available and given (abstractly) to whoever offered himself up to them. The only "emotional element" capable of being shared, while escaping any sharing, remains the obsessive value of mortal imminence, that is to say, of time which explodes existence and liberates it ecstatically from everything in it that would remain *servile*. The illusion of Acéphale is therefore the illusion of abandonment lived communally, the abandonment of and to the ultimate fear which gives ecstasy. Death, the death of the other, like friendship or love, clears the space of intimacy or interiority which is never (for Georges Bataille) the space of a subject, but a gliding beyond limits. "The Inner Experience" says the opposite of what it seems to say: it is a movement of contestation that, coming from the subject, devastates it, but has as a deeper origin the relationship with the other which is community itself, a community that would be nothing if it did not open the one who exposes himself to it to the infiniteness of alterity, while at the same time deciding its inexorable finitude. The community, the community of equals, which puts its members to the test of an unknown inequality, is such that it does not subordinate the one to the other, but makes them accessible to what is inaccessible in this new relationship of responsibility (of sovereignty?). Even if the community excludes the immediacy that would affirm the loss of everyone in the vanishing of communion, it proposes or imposes the knowledge (the experience, *Erfahrung*) of what cannot be known; that "beside-ourself" (the outside) which is abyss and ecstasy without ceasing to be a singular relationship.

Clearly it would be tempting and fallacious to search through *L'Expérience Intérieur* for the substitution or prolongation of what had not been able to take place, even as an attempt, in the Acéphale community. But what was in play demanded to be taken up again in the paradoxical form of a book. In a way, the instability of the illumination needed, before being able to be transmitted, to expose itself to others, not in order to reach in them a certain objective reality (which would have denatured it immediately), but to reflect itself therein by sharing itself and letting itself be contested (i.e., enounced differently, or even denounced in accordance with the refutation it carried in itself). Thus the exigency for a community did remain. By itself, ecstasy was nothing if it did not communicate itself and, first, did not give itself as the groundless ground of communication. Georges Bataille has always maintained that the Inner Experience could not take place if it was limited to a single individual who would have sufficed to carry the event, its disgrace and glory: the inner experience accomplishes itself, while at the same time persevering in incompleteness when it is shared and, in that sharing, exposes its limits, exposes itself inside the limits it proposes to transgress as if to bring out, through that transgression, the illusion or affirmation of a law that escapes anybody who would pretend to transgress it *alone*. A law which

17

does presuppose a community (an understanding or a common accord, be it the momentary accord of two singular beings, breaking with few words the impossibility of Saying which the unique trait of experience seems to contain; its sole content: to be untransmittable, which can be completed thus: the only thing worthwhile is the transmission of the untransmittable).

In other words: there is no simple experience. One needs moreover to have available the conditions without which it would not be possible (in its very impossibility), and this is where a community is necessary (the project of the "Socratic College" which could only fail and which was projected only as the last gasp of a communitarian experience incapable of realizing itself). Furthermore, "ecstasy" itself is communication, the negation of the isolated being who, at the same time as it disappears in that violent rupture, pretends to exalt or to "enrich" itself with what breaks its isolation by going as far as opening itself up to the unlimited — which statements, in truth, seem to be stated only to be contested: the isolated being is the individual, and the individual is only an abstraction, existence as it is represented by the weak minded conception of everyday liberalism. Maybe it is not necessary to have recourse to a phenomenon as difficult to define as "ecstasy" to extricate men from a praxis and a theory that mutilate them by separating them. There is political action, there is a task one may call philosophical, there is an ethical quest (the demand for a morality did not haunt Georges Bataille any less than it haunted Sartre, the difference being that for Bataille that demand had priority, while for Sartre, weighed down by the load of "Being and Nothingness," it could only be second-best, a hand-maiden, and thus, in advance, submissive).

Still, when we read (in the posthumous notes): "The object of ecstasy is the negation of the isolated being," we know that the imperfection of that answer is linked to the very form of a question put by a friend (Jean Bruno). On the contrary, there is evidence —

overpowering evidence — that ecstasy is without object, just as it is without a why, just as it challenges any certainty. One can write that word (ecstasy) only by putting it carefully between quotation marks, because nobody can know what it is about, and, above all, whether it ever took place: going beyond knowledge, implying un-knowledge, it refuses to be stated other than through random words that cannot guarantee it. Its decisive aspect is that the one who experiences it is no longer there when he experiences it, is thus no longer there to experience it. The same person (but he is no longer the same) may believe that he recaptures it in the past as one does a memory: I remember, I recall to mind, I talk or I write in a rapture that overflows and unsettles the very possibility of remembering. All mystics, the most rigorous, the most sober (and first of all Saint John of the Cross), have known that that remembrance, considered as personal, could only be doubtful, and, belonging to memory, took rank among that which demanded escape from it: extratemporal memory or remembrance of a past which has never been lived in the present (and thus a stranger to all *Erlebnis*).

THE SHARING OF THE SECRET

It is also in this sense that what was most personal could not be kept as the secret of one person alone, as it broke the boundaries of the person and demanded to be shared, better, to affirm itself as the very act of sharing. This sharing refers back to the community and is exposed in it; it can be theorized there — that is the risk it runs —becoming a truth or an object that could be owned while the community, as Jean-Luc Nancy says, maintains itself only as the place — the non-place — where nothing is owned, its secret being that it has no secret, working only at the unworking that traverses even writing, or that, in every public or private exchange of words, makes the final silence resound, the silence where, however, it is never certain that everything comes, finally, to an end. No end there where finitude reigns.

If, as the principle of community, we had the unfinishedness or incompleteness of existence, now as the mark of that which raises it up so high it risks disappearence in "ecstasy," we have the accomplishment of community in that which, precisely, limits it, we have sovereignty in that which makes it absent and null, its prolongation in the only communication which henceforth suits it and which passes through literary unsuitability, when the latter inscribes itself in works only to affirm the unworking that haunts them, even if they cannot not reach it. The absence of community puts an end to the hopes of the groups; the absence of a work which, on the contrary, needs and presupposes works so as to let them write themselves under the charm of unworking, is the turning point which, corresponding to the devastation of the war, will close an era. Georges Bataille will claim at times that, excepting *L'Histoire de L'Oeil* and *L'Essai Sur La Dépense*, everything he had written before — though he may have remembered it only partially — was but the aborted prelude of the exigency of writing. It is diurnal communication: it doubles as nocturnal communication (*Madame Edwarda, Le Petit...*) or the notes of a tormented Journal (which is being written without any view towards publication), unless nocturnal communication, that communication which does not avow itself, which antedates itself and takes its authority only from a non-existing author, opens up upon another form of community, when a small number of friends, each one singular, and with no forced relationships between them, form it in secret through the silent reading they share, becoming conscious of the exceptional event they are confronted with or dedicated to. Nothing can be said that would be equal to it. No commentary could accompany it: at best a code word (as are, by the way, Laure's pages on the Sacred, published and transmitted clandestinely) that, communicated to each as if he were the only one, does not recreate

20

the "sacred conjuration" that had once been dreamed, but which, without breaking the isolation, deepens it in a solitude lived in common and bound to an unknown responsibility (in regard to the unknown).

THE LITERARY COMMUNITY

The ideal community of literary communication. Circumstances helped (the importance of the aleatory, of chance, of the whim of history and of the encounter; the surrealists, André Breton before anyone else, had foreseen it and even theorized it prematurely). If need be, one could gather around a table (suggesting the hasty participants at a Seder) the few reader-witnesses, not all of whom were conscious of the importance of the fragile event that brought them together, compared to the formidable stakes of the war, which they were nearly all involved in at different levels and which exposed them to the certainty of a prompt disappearance. There it is: something had taken place which, for a few moments and due to the misunderstandings peculiar to singular existences, gave permission to recognize the possibility of a community established previously though at the same time already posthumous: nothing of it would remain, which saddened the heart while also exalting it, like the very ordeal of effacement writing demands.

Georges Bataille has stated with simplicity (with too much simplicity, maybe, but he was conscious of that) the two moments when, in his eyes, or to his mind, the exigencies for a community impose themselves in relation to the inner experience. When he writes, "my conduct with my friends has its motivations: each being, left to himself, is, I believe, incapable of going to the limits of being," this statement implies that the *experience* could not take place for the single being because its characteristic is to break up the particularity of a particular person and to expose the latter to someone else; to be therefore essentially for the other: "If I want

21

my life to have meaning for myself, it must have meaning *for someone else.*" Or: "I may not, even for a single moment, stoop to provoking myself to the extreme and cannot differentiate between myself and those among the others with whom I desire to communicate." Which implies a certain confusion: sometimes, and at the same time, the experience ("going to the extreme") can be such only if it remains communicable, and it is communicable only because, in its essence, it is an opening to the outside and an opening to others, a movement which provokes a violent dissymmetry between myself and the other: the fissure and the communication.

The two moments can thus be analyzed as distinct, though they presuppose each other by destroying each other. Bataille says for example: "The community I am talking about is the one that existed virtually because of the existence of Nietzsche (who is its exigency) and which each of Nietzsche's readers undoes by slipping away — that is to say, by not resolving the stated enigma (by not reading it)." But there was a great difference between Bataille and Nietzsche. Nietzsche had the ardent desire to be heard, but also at times the proud certainty of carrying within himself a truth too dangerous or too superior to be welcomed. For Bataille, friendship is a part of "the sovereign operation"; it is not by some whim that *Le Coupable* has as its first subtitle *L'Amitié*; friendship, it is true, is difficult to define: friendship for oneself all the way to dissolution; friendship of the one for the other, as passage and as affirmation of a continuity that takes off from the necessary discontinuity. But reading — the unworking labor of the work — is not absent from it, though it belongs at times to the vertigo of drunkenness: ". . . I had already imbibed much wine. I asked X to read a passage from the book I was carrying around with me and he read it aloud (nobody, to my knowledge, reads with a more hard-edged simplicity, with a more passionate grandeur then he). I was too drunk and no longer remember the exact passage. He himself had drunk as much as I had. It would be a mistake to think that such a reading

given by men intoxicated with drink is but a provocative paradox . . . . I believe we are united in this, that we are both open,
defenseless — through temptation — to forces of destruction, but
not like the reckless, rather like children whom a cowardly naiveté
never abandons." This, Nietzsche would probably never have
approved of: he abandons himself — the collapse — only at the
moment of madness, and that abandonment prolongs itself by
betraying itself through movements of megalomaniac compensa-
tion. The scene Bataille describes to us, whose participants are
known to us (but that is of no importance) and which was not
destined to be published (though it maintains the cautiousness of
a certain incognito: the interlocutor is not named, but he is shown
in such a way that his friends may recognize him, without naming
him; he represents friendship as much as the friend), is followed
(dated on a different day) by this statement: "A god does not busy
himself." This not-doing is one of the aspects of the unworking,
and friendship, with the reading in drunkenness, is the very form
of the "unworking community" Jean-Luc Nancy has asked us to
reflect upon, though it is not permitted to us to stop there.

I will however come back to it (some day or other). But before
that it is necessary to recall that the reader *is not a simple reader*,
free in regard to what he reads. He is desired, loved and perhaps
intolerable. He cannot know what he knows, and he knows more
than he knows. He is a companion who gives himself over to
abandonment, who is himself lost and who at the same time remains
at the edge of the road the better to disentangle what is happening
and which therefore escapes him. That is, perhaps, what these
feverish texts state: "My fellow creatures! my friends! like airless
houses with dusty windows: eyes closed, lids open!" And a bit further
on: "The one for whom I write (to whom I say *tu*), out of compassion
for what he has just read, will need to weep, then he will laugh,
for he will have recognized himself." But, afterwards, this: "If I
could know — see and discover — 'the one for whom I write,' I
think I would die. He would despise me, worthy of me. But I would

not die from his contempt: survival needs gravity."[8] These move-ments are contradictory only in appearance: "The one for whom I write" is the one whom one cannot know, he is the unknown, and the relationship with the unknown, even in writing, exposes me to death or finitude, that death which does not have it in it to appease death. What then about friendship? *Friendship: Friendship for the unknown without friends*. Or, moreover, if friendship calls upon the community through writing, it can only except itself (*friendship for the exigency of writing which excludes all friendship*). But why this "contempt"? "Worthy of me" he who, if we admit that he is a living singularity, will have to stoop to the extremes of lowness, that is to say to the experience of the only unworthiness that will make him worthy of me: in a way this would be the sovereignty of evil or the dethroned sovereignty that can no longer be shared and that, expressing itself through contempt, will attain to that depreciation which lets live or survive. "Hypocrite! To write, to be sincere and naked, nobody can do that. I don't want to do it" (*Le Coupable*). And at the same time, in the opening pages of the same book: "These notes link me like Ariadne's thread to my fellow creatures and the rest seems vanity to me. However I cannot give them to any of my friends to read." For that would mean personal reading by personal friends. Thus the anonymity of the book which does not address anybody and which, through its relationship with the unknown, initiates what Georges Bataille (at least once) will call "the negative community: the community of those who have no community."

THE HEART OR THE LAW

One can say that what designates itself — denounces itself — in these apparently confused notes, are the boundaries of thought without boundaries that needs the "I" to break itself sovereignly and that needs the exclusion of that sovereignty to open itself to a communication that cannot be shared because it involves the very suppression of the community. There is here a desperate movement to sovereignly deny sovereignty (always sullied by the emphasis that is spoken or lived by a single man in whom all the others are "incarnate") and to gain, through the impossible community (the community of/with the impossible), the possibility of a major communication, "linked to the suspension of what is nonetheless the basis of communication." Now, "the basis of communication" is not necessarily speech, or even the silence that is its foundation and punctuation, but the exposure to death, no longer my own exposure, but someone else's, whose living and closest presence is already the eternal and unbearable absence, an absence that the travail of deepest mourning does not diminish. And it is in life itself that that absence of someone else has to be met. It is with that absence — its uncanny presence, always under the prior threat of a disappearance — that friendship is brought into play and lost at each moment, a relation without relation or without relation other than the incommensurable (concerning which there is no ground to ask oneself if one has to be *sincere* or not, truthful or not, faithful or not, given that it represents the always prior absence of links or the infiniteness of abandonment). Such is, such would be the friendship that discovers the unknown we ourselves are, and the meeting of our own solitude which, precisely, we cannot be alone to experience ("incapable, by myself alone, of going to the limits of the extreme").

"The infiniteness of abandonment," "the community of those who have no community." Here perhaps we touch upon the ultimate form of the communitarian experience, after which there will be nothing left to say, because it has to know itself by ignoring itself. It is not a question of withdrawing incognito or in secret. If it is true that Georges Bataille had the feeling (especially before the war) of being abandoned by his friends, if, later, during a few months (*Le Petit*), illness forced him to remain aloof, if, in a way, he lives solitude all the more deeply in that he is unable to bear it, he knows all the better that the community is not destined to heal or protect him from it, but that it is the way in which it exposes him to it, not by chance, but as the heart of fraternity: the heart or the law.

II

THE COMMUNITY OF LOVERS

The sole law of abandonment, like the law of love,
is to be without return and without recourse.
— J.L. Nancy

I introduce here, in a way that may seem arbitrary, some pages written with no other thought than to accompany the reading of a relatively recent *récit* (but the date doesn't matter) by Marguerite Duras.[9] Without a clear idea, at any rate, that that *récit* (sufficient in itself, which is to say perfect, which is to say without a way out) would lead me back to the thought, followed up elsewhere, that questions our world — the world which is ours for being nobody's — out of the forgetting, not of the communities that survive therein (they are multiplying, in fact), but of the "communitarian" exigency that perhaps haunts them, but that almost certainly renounces itself in them.

MAY '68   May '68 has shown that without project, without conjuration, in the suddenness of a happy meeting, like a feast that breached the admitted and expected social norms, *explosive communication* could affirm itself (affirm itself beyond the usual forms of affirmation) as the opening that gave permission to everyone, without distinction of class, age, sex or culture, to mix with the first comer as if with an already loved being, precisely because he was the unknown-familiar.

"Without project": that was the characteristic, all at once distressing and fortunate, of an incomparable form of society that remained elusive, that was not meant to survive, to set itself up, not even via the multiple "committees" simulating a disordered-order, an imprecise specialization. Contrary to "traditional revolutions," it was not a question of simply taking power to replace it with some other power, nor of taking the Bastille or the Winter Palace, or the Elysée or the National Assembly, all objectives of no importance. It was not even a question of overthrowing an old world; what mattered was to let a possibility manifest itself, the possibility — beyond any utilitarian gain — of a *being-together* that gave back to all the right to equality in fraternity through a freedom of speech that elated everyone. Everybody had something to say, and, at times, to write (on the walls); what exactly, mattered little. Saying it was more important than what was said. Poetry was an everyday affair. "Spontaneous" communication, in the sense that it seemed to hold back nothing, was nothing else than communication communicating with its transparent, immediate self, in spite of the fights, the debates, the controversies, where calculating intelligence expressed itself less than a nearly pure effervescence (at any rate an effervescence without contempt, neither highbrow nor lowbrow). Because of that one could have the presentiment that with authority overthrown or, rather, neglected, a sort of *communism* declared itself, a communism of a kind never experienced before and which no ideology was able to recuperate or claim as its own. No serious attempts at reforms, but an innocent presence (supremely uncanny because of that) which, in the eyes of the men of power and eluding their analyses, could only be put down with typical sociological phrases such as *chienlit* [ragtag, mess, etc. from

30

chie-en-lit, shits in bed], that is to say the carnavalesque redoubling of their own disarray, the disarray of a command that no longer commanded anything, not even itself, contemplating, without seeing it, its own inexplicable ruin.

An innocent presence, a "common presence" (René Char), ignoring its limits, political because of its refusal to exclude anything and its awareness that it was, as such, the immediate-universal, with the impossible as its only challenge, but without determined political wills and therefore at the mercy of any sudden push by the formal institutions against which it refused to react. It is that absence of reaction (Nietzsche could be said to be its inspiration) which permitted the adverse manifestation to develop and which it would have been easy to prevent or to fight. Everything was accepted. The impossibility of recognizing an enemy, of taking into account a particular form of adversity, all that was vivifying while hastening the resolution, though there was nothing to be resolved, given that the event had taken place. The event? And had it taken place?

PRESENCE OF
THE PEOPLE

That was, and still is, the ambiguity of presence — understood as instantly realized utopia — and therefore without future, therefore without present: in suspension as if to open time to a beyond of its usual determinations. Presence of the people? Recourse to that complacent word was already abusive. Or else it had to be understood not as the totality of social forces, ready to make particular political decisions, but as their instinctive refusal to accept any power, their absolute mistrust in identifying with a power to which they would delegate themselves, thus mistrust in their declaration of impotence. Hence the ambiguity of the committees that multiplied (and of which I have already spoken), pretending to organize disorganization while respecting the latter, and that were not supposed to distinguish

31

themselves from the "anonymous and innumerable crowd, from the people spontaneously demonstrating" (Georges Préli).[10] Thus the actionless action-committees' difficulty of being, or that of the circles of friends who disavowed their previous friendship in order to call upon *friendship* (camaraderie without preliminaries) vehiculated by the requirement of being there, not as a person or subject, but as the demonstrators of a movement fraternally anonymous and impersonal.

Presence of the "people" in their limitless power which, in order not to limit itself, accepts *doing nothing*: I believe that in the still contemporary period there has not been a clearer example than the one that affirmed itself with sovereign amplitude when, to walk in procession for the dead of Charonne, an immobile, silent crowd gathered, whose number there was no reason to count because there was nothing to be added, nothing to be subtracted: it was there as a whole, not to be counted, not to be numbered, not even as a closed totality, but as an integrality surpassing any whole, imposing itself calmly beyond itself. A power supreme, because it included, without feeling diminished, its virtual and absolute powerlessness, symbolized accurately by the fact that it was there as an extension of those who could no longer be there (those assassinated at Charonne): the infinite answering the call of the finitude and prolonging it while opposing it. I believe that a form of community happened then, different from the one whose character we had thought to have defined, one of those moments when communism and community meet up and ignore that they have realized themselves by losing themselves immediately. It must not last, it must have no part in any kind of duration. That was understood on that exceptional day: nobody had to give the order to disband. Dispersal happened out of the same necessity that had gathered the innumerable. Separation was instantaneous, without any remainder, without any of those nostalgic sequels that alter the true demonstration by pretending to carry on as combat groups. The people are not like that. They are there, then they are no longer there; they ignore the structure that could stabilize them. Presence and absence, if not merged, at least exchange themselves virtually. That is what makes them formidable for the holders of a power that does not acknowledge them: not letting themselves be grasped, being as much the dissolution of the social fact as the stubborn obstinacy to reinvent the latter in a sovereignty the law cannot circumscribe, as it challenges it while maintaining itself as its foundation.

THE WORLD OF LOVERS

Assuredly there exists an abyss no rhetorical deceit can bridge between the impotent power of what one cannot refer to except by that so easily misunderstood word — the people (do not translate it as *Volk*) — and the strangeness of that antisocial society or association, always ready to dissolve itself, formed by *friends* or *couples*. Certain traits however distinguish them while bringing them together: the people (above all if one avoids sacralizing them) are not the State, not any more than they are the society in person, with its functions, its laws, its determinations, its exigencies which constitute its most proper finality. Inert, immobile, less a gathering than the always imminent dispersal of a presence momentarily occupying the whole space and nevertheless without a place (utopia), a kind of messianism announcing nothing but its autonomy and its *unworking* (on the condition that it be left to itself, or else it will change immediately and become a network of forces ready to break loose): thus are mankind's people whom it is permissible to consider as the bastardized imitation of God's people (rather similar to what could have been the gathering of the children of Israel in view of the Exodus if they had gathered while at the same time forgetting to leave), or else making them the same as "the arid solitude of the anonymous forces" (Régis Debray). That "arid solitude" is precisely

33

what justifies the comparison with what Georges Bataille has called "the true world of lovers," sensitive as he was to the antagonism between ordinary society and "the sly loosening of the social bond" implied by such a world that is, precisely, the oblivion of the world: the affirmation of a relationship so singular between beings that love itself is not necessary for it, as love, which by the way is never a certainty, may impose its requirements on a circle where its obsessions can go so far as taking on the form of the impossibility of loving: be it the unfelt, uncertain torment of those who, having lost "the intelligence of love" (Dante), however still want to tend towards the only beings whom they cannot approach by any living passion.

THE MALADY OF DEATH

Is it this torment which Marguerite Duras has called "the malady of death"? When I set out to read her book, attracted by this enigmatic title, I did not know the answer and luckily I can say that I still do not know it. That gives me the permission to take up again, as if for the first time, the reading and its commentary, both illuminating and obscuring each other. To begin with, what about that title, *The Malady of Death*, which, coming perhaps from Kierkegaard, seems to hold or guard its secret all by itself? Once pronounced, everything has been said without one's knowing what there is to be said as it is not measurable on the scales of knowledge. Diagnosis or verdict? There is something outrageous in its sobriety. It is the outrage of evil. Evil (moral or physical) is always excessive. It is the unbearable which does not permit itself to be questioned. Evil, in its excessiveness, evil as "the malady of death," cannot be limited to a conscious or unconscious "I"; it concerns first of all the other, and the other — someone else — is the innocent, the child, the sick person, whose complaint echoes as the "unheard of" scandal, because it exceeds understanding, while pledging me to respond to it without my having the power to do so.

34

These remarks do not make us stray from the text proposed, or rather imposed — for it is a declarative text and not a *récit*, even though it appears as such. Everything is decided by an initial "you" that is more than authoritarian, that summons and determines what is going to happen or what could happen to the one who has fallen into the trap of an inexorable fate. For convenience, let us say that it is the "you" of the director giving indications to the actor who has to pull the fleeting figure he will incarnate out of nothing. So be it. But then it has to be understood as coming from the supreme director: the biblical "You" that comes from on high and prophetically fixes the rough outline of the plot we move through, without our knowing what has been prescribed for us.

"*You wouldn't know her, you'd have seen her everywhere at once, in a hotel, in a street, in a train, in a bar, in a book, in a film, in yourself. . . .*"[11] The "You" never addresses her, it has no power over her who is indeterminate, unknown, unreal, thus ungraspable in her passivity, absent in her slumbering and eternally fleeting presence.

A first reading will yield this simple explanation: a man, who has never known anybody but those like him, that is to say only other men who are nothing but the multiplication of himself, a man thus, and a young woman bound to him by a paid contract for a few nights, for a whole life, which has led hasty critics to talk about a prostitute though she herself makes clear that she is not, although there is a contract — a relationship that is purely contractual (marriage, money) — because she has felt from the beginning, without knowing it clearly, that, incapable of loving, he can only approach her conditionally, after concluding a transaction, just as she apparently abandons herself entirely while abandoning only that part of her that is under contract, preserving or reserving the freedom she does not alienate. From this one could conclude that the absoluteness of the relationship has been perverted from the onset and that, in a mercantile society, there is indeed commerce between beings but never a veritable "community," never a knowledge that is more than an exchange of "good" procedures, be they as extreme as is conceivable. Power relationships in which it is the one who pays or supports who is dominated, frustrated by his very power which measures only his impotence.

That impotence is in no way the banal impotence of a failing man, faced with a woman he is incapable of meeting sexually. He does everything that has to be done. She says as much with unanswerable conciseness: "It is done." Furthermore, he happens "by pure distraction" to provoke the cry of sexual jubilation, "the muted and distant rumbling of her orgasm through her breathing"; he even manages to make her say: "What happiness." But, as nothing in him corresponds to these excessive movements (or that he judges to be so), they seem unbecoming to him, he represses them, annuls them, because they are the expression of a life exhibiting itself while he is, and always has been, deprived of that life.

The lack of feeling, the lack of love, it is that, then, which signifies death, that lethal illness that smites unjustly the one while apparently sparing the other, even though she is its messenger and as such, not without responsibility. A conclusion that disappoints us, however, insofar as it keeps to explicable givens and even though the text invites it.

In truth, the text is mysterious only because it is irreducible. That, rather than its brevity, is the root of its density. Each of us makes up his own mind concerning the characters, particularly the character of the young woman whose presence-absence is such that she imposes herself nearly by going beyond the reality she adjusts herself to. In a way, she alone exists. She is described: young, beautiful, personal, under the gaze that discovers her, by the ignorant hands that conceive her while believing that they are touching her. And, lest we forget, she is the first woman for him and is therefore the first woman for all, in the imagination that makes her more real than she could be in reality — the one who is there beyond all the epithets one is tempted to attribute to her in order to fix her being-there. There remains this statement (it is true in the conditional): "*She'd have been tall. With a long body made in a single sweep, at a single stroke, as if by God himself, with the unalterable perfection of individuality.*" "As if by God himself," thus Eve or Lilith, but without a name, less so because she is anonymous than because she seems too removed for any name to suit her. Two further traits give her a reality that nothing real would suffice to limit: the fact that she is without defenses, the weakest, the most fragile, exposing herself through her body offered ceaselessly, as her face is, a face which in its absolute visibility is its own invisible evidence — thus beckoning murder ("*strangulation, rape, ill usage, insults, shouts of hatred, the unleashing of deadly and unmitigated passions*"), but, due to her very weakness, due to her very frailty, she cannot be killed, preserved as she is by the interdiction which makes her untouchable in her constant nakedness, the closest and most distant nakedness, the inaccessible intimacy of the outside ("*you look at this shape, and as you do so you realize its infernal power* [Lilith], *its abominable frailty, its weakness, the unconquerable strength of its incomparable weakness*").

The other trait of her presence — which makes for her being there and for her not being there — is the fact that she nearly always sleeps, her sleep not even interrupted by the words that come from her, by the questions she does not have the power to ask and above all by the last judgment she utters and with which she announces that "malady of death" that constitutes his only fate — not a death to come, but a death outstripped from the beginning, as it is the abandonment of a life that has never been present. We have to understand this accurately (it is a question of understanding rather than of overhearing it unbeknownst to us): we are not face to face with this, alas, ordinary truth: I die without having lived, having never done anything but dying while living, or ignoring that death that is life reduced to me alone and lost in advance, in a lack that is impossible to perceive (the theme,

37

perhaps, of Henry James's short story, "The Beast in the Jungle," translated and staged some time ago by Marguerite Duras: "He had been the man to whom nothing was to happen.").

"And she, in the room, sleeps on. Sleeps, and you (the implacable 'you' that either establishes or holds the man it addresses within an obligation prior to all law) *don't wake her. As her sleep goes on, sorrow grows in the room . . . . She goes on sleeping, evenly . . . ."* A mysterious sleep that has to be deciphered, just as it has to be respected, that is her way of life and prevents one from knowing anything about her, except for her presence-absence which is not unrelated to the wind, to the closeness of the sea the man describes to her and whose whiteness is indistinguishable from that of the huge bed which is the unlimited space of her life, her domain and momentary eternity. To be sure, at times one thinks of Proust's Albertine to whom the narrator — scrutinizing her slumber — was closest when she was asleep, because then the distance preserving her from the lies and vulgarity of life, permitted an ideal communication — only ideal, it is true, and thus reduced to the vain beauty, the pointless purity of the idea.

But unlike Albertine, and yet perhaps also like her, if one thinks of Proust's not unveiled fate, this young woman is forever separate because of the suspect closeness with which she offers herself, her difference which is that of another species, of another type, or that of the absolutely other. (*"All you know is the grace of the bodies of the dead, the grace of those like yourself. Suddenly you see the difference between the grace of the bodies of the dead and this grace here, this royalty, made of utmost weakness, which could be crushed by the merest gesture. You realize it's here, in her, that the malady of death is fomenting, that it's this shape stretched out before you that decrees the malady of death."*) A strange passage, leading us almost abruptly to another version, another reading: "the malady of death" is no longer the sole responsibility of the one — the man — who ignores the feminine, or, even knowing it, does not know it. The malady foments itself also (or first) in her who is present and who decrees it by her very existence.

Let us proceed further in the search for (and not the elucidation of) that enigma that becomes all the darker as we pretend to bring it to the light of day, as if we, as readers, or worse, as explicators, believed ourselves exempt from the malady with which, one way or another, we are grappling. One could certainly say that what is specific to the man whose "you" determines what he must do is precisely that he is nothing except a constant "doing." If the woman is sleep, her passivity a welcoming, an offering, a surrender — and yet, in her excessive fatigue, such that she alone really talks — he, who is never described, never seen, is always coming or going, always in action in front of this body he looks upon in unhappiness, because he cannot see all of it, its impossible totality, all its aspects; though she be a "closed form" only in as much as she escapes the summons, she escapes what would turn her into a graspable whole, a sum that would integrate the infinite and thus reduce it to an integratable finite. Maybe that is the meaning of that combat always lost in advance. She sleeps, while he is refusal of sleep, impatience incapable of rest, the insomniac who would keep his eyes open in the grave, awaiting a wakening not promised him. If Pascal's words are true, one could say that of the two protagonists it is he who in his attempt to love, in his ceaseless search, is the worthier, the one closer to that absolute he finds in not finding it. He should be given that at least: his tenaciousness in trying to break out of himself, without however overstepping the norms of his own anomaly in which she sees only a redoubling of egoism (which may be too hasty a judgment), this propensity to shed tears in vain, as he does, and to which she responds dryly: "*Don't cry, it's pointless, give up the habit of weeping for yourself, it's pointless,*" while the sovereign "you" which seems to know the secret of things, says: "*You think you weep because you can't love. You weep because you can't impose death.*"

What then is the difference between these two destinies, one of which pursues a love refused to him while the other, through grace, is made for love, knows everything about love, judges and condemns those who fail in their attempt to love, but herself only offers herself to be loved (under contract) without ever giving any sign of her ability to go from passivity to limitless passion? Maybe it is that dissymmetry which arrests the reader's investigation because it also escapes the author: an inscrutable mystery.

ETHICS
AND LOVE

Is it the same dissymmetry that, according to Levinas, marks the irreciprocity of the ethical relationship between the other and me, I who am never on equal terms with the Other, an inequality measured by this impressive thought: The other is always closer to God than I am (whatever meaning one gives that name that names the unnamable)? This is not certain, and neither is it clear. Love may be a stumbling block for ethics, unless love simply puts ethics into question by imitating it. Likewise the distribution of the human between male and female creates problems in the various versions of the Bible. It is well known, and there was no need to wait for Bizet to learn that "love has never known any law." Is this therefore a return to the wilderness that does not even transgress prohibitions, given that it ignores them, or to the "anogistic" (Hölderlin) which unsettles any social relationship, just or unjust, and, contumacious to any third party, cannot be satisfied with a society of two where the reciprocity of the "I-you" would reign, but prefers to invoke the original, precreational chaos, the night without end, the outside, the fundamental unhinging? (For the Greeks, according to Phaedrus, Love is nearly as ancient as Chaos.)

The beginning of an answer can be found here: "*You ask how loving can happen — the emotion of loving. She answers: Perhaps through a lapse in the logic of the universe. She says: Through a mistake, for instance. She says: Never through an act of will.*" Let us be content with this knowledge which "knows how" to be it. What does it announce? That in the homogeneity — the affirmation of the Same — understanding demands that the heterogeneous appear suddenly, i.e., the absolute Other in terms of which any relationship signifies: no relationship, the impossibility that willing and perhaps even desire ever cross the uncrossable, in the sudden clandestine meeting (outside of time) that annuls itself with the devastating feeling that is never certain to be experienced by the one whom this movement consigns to the other perhaps by depriving him of his "self." A devastating feeling that is, in truth, beyond all feeling, ignoring pathos, overflowing consciousness, breaking with self-involvement and demanding — without rights — that which removes itself from all demands, because in my request there is not only the beyond of what could satisfy it, but the beyond of what is requested. An overbidding, an outrage of life that cannot be contained within life which thus, interrupting the pretension of always persevering in being, opens to the strangeness of an interminable dying or of an endless "error."

This is also what the oracle suggests when, in the text, it adds to the previous answers (answers to the always repeated question, "*Where does the emotion of loving spring from?*") this ultimate rejoinder: "*From anything . . . from the approach of death . . . .*" Thus returns the duplicity of the word death,[12] of that malady of death which at times would designate love prevented and at other times the pure movement of loving, both calling to the abyss, to the black night discovered by the vertiginous emptiness "of the spread legs" (how not to think here of *Madame Edwarda*?).

TRISTAN
AND ISOLDE

No end, then, to a *récit* that also says in its own way: no more *récit*, and yet an end, perhaps a remission, perhaps a final condemnation. For it so happens that one day the young woman is no longer there. A disappearance that cannot surprise, as it is but the exhaustion of an appearance that gave itself only in sleep. She is no longer there, but so discreetly, so absolutely, that her absence suppresses her absence, so that to look for her is pointless, just as it would be impossible to recognize her and that to join her, be it only in the thought that she has existed only through the imagination, cannot interrupt the solitude where the testamentary word is murmured endlessly: the malady of death. And here are the last words (are they the last?): "*Soon you give up, don't look for her anymore, either in the town or at night or in the daytime: Even so you have managed to live that love in the only way possible for you. Losing it before it happened.*" A conclusion which in its admirable density may state, not the failure of love in a singular case, but the fulfillment of all veritable love which would consist in realizing itself exclusively according to the mode of loss, that is to say realizing itself by losing not what has belonged to you but what one has never had, for the "I" and the "other" do not live in the same time, are never together (synchronously), can therefore not be contemporary, but separated (even when united) by a "not yet" which goes hand in hand with an "already no longer." Isn't it Lacan who said (maybe an inaccurate quotation): to desire means to give what one does not have to someone who does not want it? Which does not mean that love can be lived only according to a mode of expectation or nostalgia, terms too easily reducible to a psychological register, while the relationship that is at stake here is not *mundane*, given that it presupposes the disappearance, even the collapse, of the world. Let us remember Isolde's words: "We have lost the world, and the world, us." And let us also remember that even the reciprocity of the love relationship, as Tristan and Isolde's story represents it,

42

the paradigm of shared love, excludes simple mutuality as well as a unity where the Other would blend with the Same. And this brings us back to the foreboding that passion eludes possibility, eluding, for those caught by it, their own powers, their own decision and even their "desire," in that it is strangeness itself, having consideration neither for what they can do nor for what they want, but luring them into a strangeness where they become estranged from themselves, into an intimacy which also estranges them from each other. And thus, eternally separated, as if death was in them, between them? Not separated, not divided: inaccessible and, in the inaccessible, in an infinite relationship.

That is what I read in this *récit* devoid of anecdote where impossible love (no matter its origin) can be translated by an analogy with the first words of an ethics (words Levinas has uncovered for us): an infinite attention to the Other, as for the one whose destitution puts him above all and any being, an urgent and ardent obligation that makes one dependent, takes one "hostage," and, Plato already has said it, makes one a slave beyond any form of admitted servility. But is morality law and does passion defy all law? That is precisely what Levinas does not say, contrary to some of his commentators. An ethics is possible only when — with ontology (which always reduces the Other to the Same) taking the backseat — an anterior relation can affirm itself, a relation such that the self is not content with recognizing the Other, with recognizing itself in it, but feels that the Other always puts it into question to the point of being able to respond to it only through a responsibility that cannot limit itself and that exceeds itself without exhausting itself. A responsibility or obligation towards the Other that does not come from the Law but from which the latter would derive in what makes it irreducible to all forms of legality through which one necessarily tries to regulate it, while at the same time pronouncing it the exception or the extra-ordinary which cannot be enounced in any already formulated language.[13]

THE LETHAL LEAP

Thus: an obligation which is not an agreement in the name of the Law, but is as if anterior to being and to freedom, where the latter is indistinguishable from spontaneity. "I" am not free towards the other if I am always free to decline the exigency that sets me off from myself and excludes me at the limit of myself. But doesn't that apply to passion? The latter pledges us fatally and, as if in spite of ourselves, to another who attracts us all the more in that he seems beyond the possibility of ever being rejoined, being so far beyond everything that matters to us.

This leap that is affirmed by love — symbolized by Tristan's prodigious bound onto Isolde's bed such that no earthly trace of their coming together remains — evokes the "lethal leap" which, according to Kierkegaard, is necessary to elevate oneself to the ethical and, above all, religious level. A lethal leap that will take shape in the following question: "Does a man have the right to let himself be put to death in the name of truth?" In the name of truth? This creates a problem: what if it is for someone else, for helping someone else? The answer is already given in Plato, with the strength of simplicity, when Phaedrus says: "There is no doubt, to die for someone else is something only those who love consent to." And then quotes the example of Alcestis who through sheer tenderness took the place of her husband (it really is the "substitution" of "the one for the other") to save him from the death penalty. Now it is true that Diotima (who, as a woman and foreigner, has the supreme knowledge of Love) will immediately rejoin that Alcestis has in no way asked to die *for* her husband but to acquire, through a sublime act, the renown that will make her immortal in her very death. Not that she did not love, but love has no other object than immortality. Which puts us on the oblique path love opens as a dialectical means to journey by leaps and bounds all the way to the highest spirituality.

44

No matter the importance of platonic love, that child of avid and twisted resource, one clearly feels that Phaedrus's conception has not been rebutted. Love, stronger than death. Love which does not suppress death but which oversteps the limit death represents and thus renders it powerless in regard to helping someone else (that infinite movement that carries towards him and, in that tension, leaves no time to come back and worry about "oneself"). Not so as to glorify death by glorifying love, but, perhaps on the contrary, to give to life a transcendency without glory that puts it endlessly at the service of the other.

I do not say that that way ethics and passion become one and the same. Passion retains as its characteristic the fact that its movement, difficult to resist, does not upset spontaneity, nor the *conatus*, but is on the contrary what outbids them, what can go all the way to destruction. And must one not at least add that to love is surely to have in sight the other alone, not as such, but as the unique that eclipses and annuls all the others? Therefore excess is its only measure while violence and nocturnal death cannot be excluded from the exigency to love. As Marguerite Duras reminds us: "*The wish to be about to kill a lover, to keep him for yourself, yourself alone, to take him, steal him in defiance of every law, every moral authority — you don't know what that is . . .?*" No, he doesn't know. And thus the implacable and contemptuous verdict: "*A dead man's a strange thing.*"

He does not answer. I will be careful not to answer in his stead, or else, coming back yet again to the Greeks, I would murmur: But I know who you are. Not the celestial or Uranian Aphrodite whom only the love of souls (or of boys) can satisfy, nor the terrestrial or popular Aphrodite who still wants bodies and even women, so that, through them, he be engendered; neither only the one, nor only the other; but you are also the third, the one least named, the most feared and, because of that, the most loved, the one who hides behind the other two from which she is

45

inseparable: the Chthonic or underground Aphrodite who belongs to death[14] towards which she leads those she chooses or who let themselves be chosen, uniting, as one sees here, the sea from which she is born (and does not stop being born), the night which signifies perpetual sleep and the silent injunction addressed to the "community of lovers," so that the latter, responding to the impossible exigency, expose themselves and one for the other to death's dispersal. A death, by definition, without glory, without consolation, without recourse, which no other disappearance can equal, except perhaps for that disappearance that inscribes itself in writing, when the work which is its drifting is from the onset the renunciation of *creating a work,* indicating only the space in which resounds, for all and for each, and thus for nobody, the always yet to come words of the unworking.

> Through the venom of immortality
> women's passion comes to completion
> (Marina Tsetaieva, *Eurydice to Orpheus*)

TRADITIONAL COMMUNITY, ELECTIVE COMMUNITY

The community of lovers. This romantic title that I have given those pages, in which there is neither a shared relationship nor definite lovers, is it not paradoxical? Certainly. But this paradox confirms perhaps the extravagance of what one seeks to designate by the name of *community?* At the onset there is need to distinguish — with whatever difficulty — between traditional community and elective community. (The first is imposed on us without our having the liberty of choice in the matter: it is *de facto* sociality, or the glorification of the earth, of blood, or even of race. But what about the other? One calls it elective in the sense that it exists only through a decision that gathers its members around a choice without which it could not have taken place; is that choice free? or, at least, does that freedom suffice to express, to affirm the sharing that is the truth of this community?) Likewise one may question that which would permit one to speak without equivocation of the community of lovers. Georges Bataille wrote: "If this world were not endlessly crisscrossed by the convulsive movements of beings in search of each other . . ., it would appear like an object of derision offered to those it gives birth to." But what about those "convulsive" movements called upon to give value to the world? Is it a question of the love (happy or unhappy) that forms a society within society and from which the latter receives its right to be known as legal or conjugal society? Or is it a movement that cannot abide any name — neither love nor desire — but that attracts the beings in order to throw them towards each other (two by two or more, collectively), according to their body or according to their heart and thought, by tearing them from ordinary society? In the first case (let us define it too simply as conjugal love) it is clear that the "community of lovers" attenuates its own exigency through the compromise it establishes with the collectivity which permits it to last by making it renounce what characterizes it: its secret behind which hides "execrable excesses."[15] In the second case, the community of lovers no longer cares about the forms of the tradition or any social agreement, be it the most permissive. From that point of view, the so-called "*maisons closes*" ("closed houses," brothels) or their surrogates do not, anymore than Sade's chateaux, constitute a marginality able to undermine society. On the contrary — and because such specialized places remain legal and all the more so if they are forbidden. It is not because Madame Edwarda is a young woman exhibiting herself in a manner that is, all in all, rather banal, by exhibiting her sex as the most sacred part of her being, that she breaks with our world or with any world; it is rather because that exhibition conceals her by handing her over to an ungraspable singularity (one can literally no longer grasp her) and that thus,

47

with the complicity of the man who loves her momentarily with an infinite passion, she *abandons herself* — it is in this that she symbolizes sacrifice — to the first comer (the chauffeur) who does not know, who will never know that he is in touch with what is most divine or with the absolute that rejects any assimilation.

THE DESTRUCTION
OF SOCIETY,
APATHY

The community of lovers — no matter if the lovers want it or not, enjoy it or not, be they linked by chance, by "*l'amour fou*," by the passion of death (Kleist) — has as its ultimate goal the destruction of society. There where an episodic community takes shape between two beings who are made or who are not made for each other, a war machine is set up or, to say it more clearly, the possibility of a disaster carrying within itself, be it in infinitesimal doses, the menace of universal annihilation. This is the level at which one has to consider the "scenario" that imposed itself on Marguerite Duras and which of necessity implicates her, given that she has imagined it. The two beings shown us represent, without joy, without happiness, and as separate as they seem to be, the hope of singularity which they can share with no one else, not only because they are locked up, but also because in their common indifference, they are locked up together with death which the one reveals to the other as that which he incarnates and as the blow she would like to receive from him, as sign of the passion she expects in vain from him. By creating this character who is forever separated from the feminine, even when he couples with a chance woman to whom he gives a pleasure he does not share, Marguerite Duras has, in a way, sensed that it was necessary to go beyond the magnetized circle representing with too much complacency the romantic union of lovers, even if the latter's blind motivation comes more from the need for losing themselves than from any concern with finding themselves. And yet she reproduces one of the eventualities that Sade's imagination (and his very life) has offered us as the banal example of the play of passions. *Apathy*, impassibility, the non-event of feelings and all forms of impotence, not only do not prevent relationships between beings, but lead those relationships towards crime which is the ultimate and (if one may say so) incandescent form of insensibility. But, precisely, in the *récit* that we are turning around and around as if trying to wring out its secret, death is summoned and simultaneously devalorized, the impotence being such that it cannot reach that far, either because it would seem too measured or, on the contrary, because it reaches an excess even Sade is unaware of.

Here is the room, the closed space open to nature and closed to other humans where, during an indefinite time reckoned in nights — though no night may come to an end — two beings try to unite only to live (and in a certain way to celebrate) the failure that constitutes the truth of what would be their perfect union, the *lie* of that union which always takes place by not taking place. Do they, in spite of all that, form some kind of *community*? It is rather *because* of that that they form a community. They are side by side, and that contiguity, passing through every form of empty intimacy, preserves them from playing the comedy of a "fusional or communional" understanding. A prison community, organized by the one, consented to by the other, where what is at stake is indeed the attempt to love — but for Nothing, an attempt that has in the end no other object than that nothing which animates them unbeknownst to themselves and exposes them to nothing else than to touching each other in vain. Neither joy nor hatred, a solitary *jouissance*, solitary tears, the pressure of an implacable Superego, and finally a single sovereignty, the sovereignty of death at large, which may be evoked but not shared, that death of which one does not die, a death without power, without effect, without achievement, a death which, in the derision it offers, keeps the attraction of "inexpressible life, the only one you accept in the end to be united with" (René Char). How not to search that space where, for a time span lasting from dusk to dawn, two beings have no other reason to exist than to expose themselves totally to each other — totally, integrally, absolutely — so that their common solitude may appear not in front of their own eyes but in front of ours, yes, how not to look there and how not to rediscover "the negative community, the community of those who have no community"?

THE ABSOLUTELY FEMININE

In a certain way it should be clear that I no longer speak exactly as I should of Marguerite Duras's text. If I force myself to betray it less, I happen again upon the strangeness of the young woman who is always there, as if eternally, in her fragility, ready to welcome everything that may be *asked* of her. But having written that, I immediately realize the need to express more subtle nuances: she is also refusal, she refuses for instance to call him by his name, i.e., to make him exist nominally; just as she does not accept his tears of which she gives only a restrictive interpretation: she ignores them, protected as she is, cluttering up the whole world without leaving him the slightest space; just as, finally, she refuses to listen to his story of the child, of his childhood, through which he would like no doubt to justify — having loved his mother too much — not being able to love the latter again incestuously in her — a story that is unique for him, banal for her ("*she's heard and read it too often, everywhere, in a number of books*"). And this means that she is not able to limit herself to being a mother, a substitute for the mother, for she is beyond any specificity characterizing her as such and such. She is thus also the absolutely feminine, and yet remains *this* woman alive to the point of being close to death if he were capable of giving it to her. Thus she accepts everything from him, without ceasing to lock him in his male closure, having relationships only with other men, something she tends to designate as his "malady" or as one of the forms of that malady which in itself is much vaster.

(Homosexuality, to come to that name which is never pronounced, is not "the malady of death," it only makes it appear, in a slightly artificial way, as it is difficult to contest that all the nuances of sentiment, from desire to love, are possible between beings, be they alike or unalike). His malady? The malady of death? It is mysterious: repulsive and attractive. It is because the young woman had the foreboding that he was stricken by it or that he was stricken by a singularity as yet hard to name, that she accepted the contract, i.e., accepted locking herself in with him. She adds that she knew as soon as he spoke, but that she knew without knowing, without as yet being able to name it: "*For the first few days I couldn't put a name to it. Then I could.*" But the answers she gives concerning such a lethal illness, no matter how precise they are — and which amount to saying: he dies for not having lived, he dies without his death being death for any life (he thus does not die or his death deprives him of a lack which he will never know) — such answers have no definitive value. Even less so as it is he, the man without life, who has organized the attempt to search for life in "the knowledge of that" (of the female body: *there* existence itself resides), in the knowledge of that which incarnates life, of "*the identity between that skin and the life it contains,*" and in the risky approach of a body capable of putting children into the world (which means that she is also the mother for him even if that is not especially important to her). That is what he wants to try, to try for "*several days . . . perhaps even for your whole life.*" That is what he asks, and he clarifies his demand when answering the question: "*Try what?*": "*Loving, you answer.*" Such an answer may sound naive and touching, and proportionate to his ignorance, as if love could be born from a will-to-love (we remember her answer: "*Never through an act of will.*") and as if love, always unjustifiable, did not presuppose the unique, unforeseeable encounter. And yet, perhaps he goes further in his naivete than those who presume to know. In that fortuitous woman, with whom he wants "to try, to try," he is bound to come up against all women, their magnificence, their mystery, their realm, or, more simply, the unknown they represent, their "ultimate reality"; there are no run-of-the-mill women, it is not through the writer's arbitrary decision that this woman slowly acquires the truth of her mythic body: that is her given, and it is the gift she offers though it cannot be received, neither by him nor by anybody else, maybe only and partially by the reader. The community between these two beings, which never places itself on a psychological or sociological level, is the most astounding and yet the most evident going beyond the mythic and the metaphysical.

There are indeed relations between them: on his side, a kind of desire — a desireless desire, given that he can couple with her, which is rather or above all a desire-for-knowledge, an attempt to come close in her to that which eludes every approach, to see her as she is. And yet he does not *see* her; he feels that he never sees her (in this sense she is the anti-Beatrice, Beatrice having her being wholly in the vision one has of her, a vision that presupposes the full scale of the seeable, from the physical sight that strikes one like lightning to the absolute visibility where she is no longer distinguishable from the Absolute itself: God, and the *theos*, theory, the ultimate of what can be seen) — and, at the same time, she inspires no repugnance in him, only a *relation* of apparent insensibility that is not indifference, since it calls forth tears upon tears. And maybe insensibility opens the man who believes that he does not go beyond it to a pleasure one cannot name: "*Perhaps you get from her a pleasure you have never known before, I don't know.*" (Thus the supreme jurisdiction cannot pronounce itself: pleasure is essentially that which escapes); in the same way it opens up solitude for him: he does not know whether this new body he reaches, without being able to reach it, lessens his solitude or, on the contrary, whether it creates it: previously he may not have known that his relationships with the others, with his fellow creatures, were perhaps also relationships of solitude, which, because of modesty, propriety, submission to custom, put aside that *excess* that comes with the feminine. Assuredly, as time passes, and in his realization that with her time no longer passes, and that thus he is deprived of his small properties, "his own room," which being inhabited seems empty — and it is the emptiness she sets up which makes it clear that she is supernumerary — as time passes he happens upon the thought that she ought to disappear and that everything would be easier if she returned to the sea (from which he believes her to have come), a thought that does not reach beyond the stray impulse to think. However, when she will really have withdrawn, he will experience a kind of regret and the desire to see her again in the new solitude her sudden absence creates. But he makes the mistake of talking to others about it or even of laughing about it, as if that attempt made with utmost seriousness, ready to give his whole life to it, left in his memory but the derisiveness of the illusory. And this is exactly one of the traits of the *community*, when that community dissolves itself, giving the impression of never having been able to exist, even when it did exist.

THE UNAVOWABLE COMMUNITY   But she herself, this young woman, so mysterious, so obvious, but whose obviousness — the ultimate reality —is never better stated than in the imminence of her disappearance, in the threat where, letting all of herself be seen, she abandons her admirable body to the point where she could instantly cease to be, at any moment, depending only on her desire (the fragility of the infinitely beautiful, the infinitely real, which, even under contract, remains without guarantee): who is she? It is too easy to get rid of her, as I have done somewhat offhandedly, by identifying her with pagan Aphrodite or with Eve and Lilith. That kind of symbolism is too facile. In any event, during the nights they spend together (it is quite true that she is essentially nocturnal) she belongs to the *community*, she is born from the community, while making felt, through her fragility, her inaccessibility and magnificence, that the strangeness of what could not be common is what founds that community, eternally temporary and always already deserted. There is no happiness here (even if she says: what joy); "*As her sleep goes on, sorrow grows in the room.*" But to the extent that the man gets a measure of glory from it, believing himself to be the king of unhappiness, he destroys its truth or authenticity, insofar as that unhappiness becomes his property, his fortune, his privilege, that over which he is entitled to weep.

However, it is not that he does not bring something to her also. He tells her the world, he tells her the sea, he tells her the time that passes and the dawn that paces her sleep. It is also he who asks the question. She is the oracle, but the oracle is an answer only through the impossibility of questioning. "*She says: Ask questions then, I can't do it on my own.*" There is, in truth, but one question, and it is the only possible question, asked in the name of all by the one who, in his solitude, does not know that he is asking in the name of all: "*You ask if she thinks anyone could love you. She says no, not possibly.*" An answer so categorical that it cannot come from an ordinary mouth, but only from very high and from very far, a superior jurisdiction that also expresses itself in him in a modicum of partial truths: "*You say that love has always struck you as out of place, you've never understood, you've always avoided loving . . .*" — remarks that turn the first question upside down and reduce it to a psychological simplification (he has voluntarily

54

kept himself outside the circle of love: he is not loved because he has always wanted to keep his *freedom* — his freedom not to love, thus committing the "Cartesian" error according to which it is the freedom of the will which, prolonging God's, cannot, must not let itself be subverted by the violence of the passions). And yet, at the same time that it admits these abrupt statements, the *récit*, so brief yet so dense, admits statements more difficult to fit into a simple doctrine. It is easy to say (he is told and in turn admits to it) that he loves nothing and nobody: just as he allows himself to admit that he has never loved a woman, that he has never desired a woman — not even once, not for a single moment. However, in the *récit* he gives proof of the contrary: he is linked to that being which is there because of a desire (a desire that may possibly be weak, but how to qualify it?) that makes her open herself to what he asks without asking. *"You know you can dispose of her in whatever way you wish, even the most dangerous"* (no doubt to kill her, which would mean making her even more real), *"You don't. Instead you stroke her body as gently as if it ran the risk of happiness . . . ."* It is a surprising relationship which revokes everything one may have said about it, and which shows the indefinable power of the feminine over what wants to, or believes it can, stay foreign to it. Not Goethe's "eternal feminine," that pale shadow of Dante's earthly and heavenly Beatrice. But without there being any trace of profanation, there remains her separate existence retaining something of the sacred, particularly when at the end she offers her body, just as the eucharistic body was offered in an absolute, immemorial gift. It is said in three solemn yet simple lines. *"She says: Take me, so it may have been done. You do so, you take her. It is done. She goes back to sleep."* After which, everything having been consummated, she is no longer there. Gone during the night, she left with the night. *"She'd never come back."*

One can dream about the disappearance. Either he could not keep her, the community coming to an end as randomly as it had begun; or else she has done her work, she has changed him more radically than he knows, leaving him the memory of a love lost before it could have come to pass. (Similarly, the disciples of Emmaus: they convince themselves of the divine presence only when it has left them.) Or else, and that is the unavowable, uniting with her according to her will, he has also given her that death she awaited, of which he was until then not capable, and which also fulfills his earthly fate — actual death or imaginary death, it does not matter. It evasively consecrates *the always uncertain end* inscribed in the destiny of the community.

The unavowable community: does that mean that it does not acknowledge itself or that it is such that no avowal may reveal it, given that each time we have talked about its way of being, one has had the feeling that one grasped only what makes it exist by default? So, would it have been better to have remained silent? Would it be better, without extolling its paradoxical traits, to live it in what makes it contemporary to a past which it has never been possible to live? Wittgenstein's all too famous and all too often repeated precept, "Whereof one cannot speak, there one must be silent" — given that by enunciating it he has not been able to impose silence on himself — does indicate that in the final analysis one has to talk in order to remain silent. But with what kinds of words? That is one of the questions this little book entrusts to others, not that they may answer it, rather that they may choose to carry it with them, and, perhaps, extend it. Thus one will discover that it also carries an exacting political meaning and that it does not permit us to lose interest in the present time which, by opening unknown spaces of freedom, makes us responsible for new relationships, always threatened, always hoped for, between what we call work, *oeuvre*, and what we call unworking, *désoeuvrement*.

NOTES

1 Jean-Luc Nancy, *La Communauté Désoeuvrée*, in *Aléa*, 4.

2 See the journal *Le Scarabée International*, 3.

3 The idea of "communal (*communielle*) unity" is not foreign to the pages on the Sacred published before the war in *Cahiers d'Art*, perhaps as accompaniment to certain of Laure's expressions. The same applies to "the Sacred is communication," a phrase that lends itself to a double interpretation. Or again, "communion, fusion, ecstasy require breaking down walls . . ." — all of that hastily jotted down in notebooks not meant for publication, which, however, one cannot neglect because of the burning, unguarded necessity they express.

4 He who is ordered according to the principle of insufficiency is also doomed to excess. Man: an insufficient being with excess as his horizon. Excess is not glut, superabundance. The excess of lack and due to lack is the never satisfied exigency of human insufficiency.

5 Concerning the word "Come," one cannot but turn the mind to Jacques Derrida's unforgettable book *D'un Ton Apocalyptique Adopté Naquèe en Philosophie* (Galilée), and particularly this sentence which has a special consonance with the one just quoted (taken from *Le Pas Au-delà*): "In its *affirmative* tone, 'Come' by itself indicates neither a desire, nor an order, nor a prayer, nor a demand." Another reflection that needs at least to be presented here: "Isn't the apocalyptic a transcendental condition of all discourse, of all experience even, of each mark, of each trace?" That would mean that the apocalyptic voice could be heard in the community, prior to any understanding and as its condition? Perhaps.

6 There is the gift by which one forces the one who receives it to give back a surplus of power or prestige to the one who gives — thus, one never gives. The gift that is abandonment commits the abandoned being to giving without any return in mind, without any calculation and without

57

any safeguard even for his own giving being: thus the exigency of the infinite that resides in the silence of abandonment.

7 Dostoevsky's novel, *The Possessed*, or *The Demons*, originates, as we know, in a minor political event, though highly significant in other respects. We also know that Freud's reflection on the origin of society makes him look into a *crime* (dreamed or fulfilled — but for Freud, of necessity, real, realized) for the passage from the horde to the regulated and ordered community. The murder of the leader of the horde turns the latter into a father, the horde into a group and its members into sons and brothers. "Crime presides over the birth of the group, of history, of language" (Eugène Enriquez, *De la Horde á l'Etat*, Gallimard). One would commit a fundamental error (so it seems at least to me) if one did not discern what separates Freud's reverie from the exigency of Acéphale: (1) Death is indeed present in Acéphale, but murder eludes it, even under its sacrificial form. To begin with, the victim is consenting, a consent that is not enough, as the only one who can give death is the one who, giving it, would die at the same time, that is, could substitute himself for the voluntary victim. (2) The community cannot found itself on the bloody sacrifice of two of its members alone, called upon (scapegoats of a sort) to expiate for all. Each person should have to die for all, and it is in the death of all that each person would determine the community's destiny. (3) But to give oneself, as a project, the execution of a sacrificial death means to break the law of the group whose first requirement is to renounce creating a *work* (even though it be the work of death) and whose essential project excludes all projects. (4) From this follows the passage to a completely different kind of sacrifice, a sacrifice that would no longer be the murder of one person or of all persons, but gift and abandonment, the infinite of abandonment. The beheading, the privation of the Head does not touch the leader or the father, does not institute the others as brothers, but brings them into play by handing them over to the "endless unfettering of the passions." Which links Acéphale to the presentiment of a disaster that would transcend all forms of transcendence.

8 Georges Bataille, *Oeuvres Complètes*, vol. 5, p. 447, Gallimard.

[9] Marguerite Duras, *La Maladie de la Mort*, Editions de Minuit: Paris, 1982. (Translated as *The Malady of Death* by Barbara Bray, Grove Press: New York, 1986.)

[10] Georges Préli, *La Force du Dehors*, Encres, Editions Recherches.

[11] The italics are the author's for all citations from the book. By these means I wish to call attention to the characteristic of a voice whose origin escapes us.

[12] By simplifying greatly, one could recognize here the confirmation of the conflict which according to Freud (a caricatured Freud, rather) breaks out implicitly or explicitly between men, makers of groups thanks to their homosexual leaning, be they sublimated or not (the S.A.), and the woman who alone can speak the truth of love, which is always "encroaching, exclusive, excessive, terrifying." The woman knows that the group, the repetition of the Same or the Similar, is in truth the grave-digger of real love which feeds only on differences. The ordinary human group, the one that acknowledges itself and is, *par excellence*, civilizing, "tends more or less to let the homogenous, the repetitive, the continuous prevail over the heterogenous, the new and the acceptance of the fissure." Woman then becomes the "intruder" who perturbs the quiet continuity of the social bond and who does not recognize the prohibition. She conspires with the unavowable. This permits us to recognize the two aspects of death according to Freud: the death instinct is at work inside civilization, insofar as the latter tends, in order to maintain itself, towards the disorder of terminal homogeneity (maximum entropy). But it is no less at work when, on the initiative and the complicity of women, the heterogeneous, exclusive alterity, violence without law, uniting Eros and Thanatos, impose themselves all the way to the end (cf. Eugène Enriquez, *De la Horde à l'Etat*).

[13] One cannot get rid of the transcendence or preeminence of the Law so quickly when the latter, according to well-known mystic views, is not only considered to have been created two thousand years before the creation of the world, but, connected to the unnamed name of God, contributes to that creation, while leaving it unfinished. Whence this

redoubtable reversal: the Law (the alliance) given to mankind to free it from idolatry risks falling into the hands of an idolatrous cult if it is adored in and for itself, without submitting itself to the unending study, to the masterful teaching its practice demands. A teaching which in turn does not dispense — no matter how indispensable it is — with renouncing its primacy when the urgency of bringing help to someone upsets all study and imposes itself as application of the Law which always precedes the Law.

[14] cf. Sarah Kofman, *Comment s'en Sortir?*, Galilée.

[15] Bataille writes violently: "The empty horror of normal conjugality already locks them in."